The Galaxy Club

The Galaxy Club

Brendan Connell

Chômu Press

The Galaxy Club

Brendan Connell
Published by Chômu Press, MMXIV

Published in February 2014 by Chômu Press.
by arrangement with the author.
All rights reserved by the author.

ISBN: 978-1-907681-25-7

First Edition

Design and layout by: Bigeyebrow and Chômu Press
Cover photograph by: Stella Connell Levy
Dragons by: Katsushika Hokusai

E-mail: info@chomupress.com
Internet: chomupress.com

for Loha

Those Underground

Phosphorous. Can still smell the colors hear the rain as it patters from our seeing countless rockets coughing mist and sulfur running out on the ground the pain of machinery, the constant bellow that swept us away. But don't think we rest, watching bonded together by a common sadness a well that sinks trillions of fathoms deep but everything stays the same stays in a way the same.

Neptune. Jaws ripped off eyeballs gone ahead so we see with our hearts or call it what you will as if we had anything left screaming out warnings that are not heard in voices that smell of corrupted fuel day after refuse crawl of snails trembling of dandelions as they try to talk tickle our noses.

We were here and he was there some river of black. The sun vomited its light above us. The trees stood still. The cars drove by. Seen through a net of clots.

Alcohol. He stood there waving his thumb at them malingering running dead it's all the same trembling in unease yes even trembling now someone might feel the ground shake.

Alfonso Torcuato Southerland-Hevia y Miranda

I am about, um, six feet tall, with brown eyes and, um, tawny hair. I had to get to the bureau, so I showered, shaved and put on a fresh shirt. Standing in front of the mirror, I did up my tie.

I am about, um, six feet tall. I am descended from Spanish grandees, though my great grandfather was a Scottish nobleman who could walk seventy miles in a day. I stared in the mirror. Everything looked alright. I turned. The curtains, of fine lace, were flawlessly parted and I could see the butt-end of my Cadillac in the driveway.

Cleopatra

Small towns are easier to be spotted in and I didn't like that. But I supposed it didn't matter because I was a long way away from anywhere anyone would care, and people are bastards everywhere, only some are a little slower than others.

I was under a sky so turquoise it almost made me sick, away from the people who took and those waiting to be taken—those who said they cared and those who I knew would just about kill me if I gave them the chance, something I had no intention of doing as I had no intention of being taken—but then maybe everyone with intention or otherwise is waiting for it, because sooner or later it happens and you find yourself lying there with your head knocked off or heart torn out. So I had hitchhiked out of Alexandria all the way to Thebes, spent the night there and forty dollars on what people call a good time but what really wasn't, what was really just a half a dozen overpriced drinks at some dive where everyone wore boots and a cheap bed and a cheaper woman who had a dirty mouth and who laughed too loud and talked too much. And that morning—early, her still in bed snoring away—I hoofed it to the highway and caught a ride as far as Edfu, a lot of poor looking houses made of mud, beat-up liquor stores, and was dropped off in front of a cemetery where a bunch of guys from Vietnam and Korea and probably some stray remains from Bataan lay buried. I stood there for about three hours with my thumb stuck out like a fool before anyone picked me up and then the old man and me drove thirty miles and he let me off in front of a place called Gilbert's Pharmacy.

I had told him I had to get my medication and see someone about some work and thanked him and shook his hand and smiled. He probably knew I was lying about the work part, but he had probably been lied to a lot in his time.

He said the name of the town, but I didn't quite catch it and didn't really care.

It was no Heliopolis though.

It was a real hole, but I had been in a lot of holes in my life, had come from a hole, would return to a hole, and so it was pretty easy. The hard part was trying to pretend like any of it really mattered, looking around at a big wide street half the buildings abandoned with roofs sinking in windows broken the other half looking like they'd go out of business any minute and some run-down looking houses an ageless man standing idly in front of one. Might as well call it rubesville.

I went into the pharmacy and got a 4 oz bottle of terps. The druggist who might or might not have been Gilbert didn't ask me to show him my driver's license or sign a piece of paper and I was telling him some line about having a bad cold but he had probably sold more of that stuff to guys like me than anyone who was actually sick.

He was gazing at me with those soft far-away eyes I had seen many times before. I thanked him in a way that meant no thanks, took the bag and left thinking about how many times I'd run, from how many people I'd run if they find you they'll kill you running under the mantle of trees every part of me soaked with sweat the gun almost slipping from my hands.

It's okay, I thought, this place is quiet and no one is following you and there's nothing to worry about if you want trouble you can surely find it but it doesn't have to be that way.

I wasn't hungry but knew I had to eat something and was ready to drink something so went into a grocery that was next door. It was an okay place, sort of small and friendly somebody nodding at me or watching me and I went in the back to the meat counter and they had some cooked pork ribs and I asked for a couple of handfuls of them. The butcher wrapped them in tinfoil and put them in a paper bag. Then I went to the liquor section and there was another man there looking at the beer which was in the cooler just across. He was about twenty-five or twenty-eight with black hair below his shoulders and a blue bandana over his forehead and some scanty whiskers on his face some astrologer probably never broke his back. I was looking at the bottles of booze trying to decide which way to go. I picked up a bottle of Seagram's Seven Crown and gazed at the label.

"That's my drink," he said.

He was grinning. Another Caesarion strangled I guess.

"Well—it's cheap enough," I said and took a few long

steps to the checkout and asked for a pack of smokes and paid and then stepped outside. I sat down on the pavement and took out one of the ribs and started eating it and it was good and full of fat remembered back in Memphis she used to cook them like that only better they tied a rope to the block us floating along on the barge and finished it and threw the bone away from me thinking some dog or hyena could have it and then stood up and stuck out my thumb and a few cars passed.

"Where are you going?"

It was the man from the liquor section. He was still grinning.

"Aswan," I said.

"That's north?"

"Yes."

He motioned towards an old Chevy truck.

"Get in, boss," he said

So I got in and he tried the ignition a few times until it took and we drove off.

His truck was one of those old rickety things without much in the way of shocks that made a lot of noise and probably broke down about every other day some broken donkey and with windows rolled down we went north for a few miles and then he wrestled with the steering wheel and turned left onto a smaller road that I knew wasn't the right one and I told him that I wasn't that way and he said he didn't care if I was laughing uneasily.

"Taking a longer way. Got to see my aunt."

I looked at him for a while and didn't say anything. I should have probably told him to stop and gotten out there. But to do something like that you actually have to care remembering my father a long time ago walking by the house he kept walking by the house there were guns going off and I put my head in the dirt could smell it. Like some kind of human ostrich.

"My name's Elmer," he said.

"What?"

"My name."

"What is it?"

"Elmer."

"Okay."

"And yours?"

"Cleopatra."

He looked at me, the grin sort of flattening out a little.

"Where are you from?" he asked.

"Around. From all around."

"I'm local."

I bet you are I thought. He had a scrawny build and I knew I could have broken him in two pretty easily remembered getting real breaking his knee cap on Fell Street and I knew he wasn't carrying a gun because I could see right through him. I had left him there on the sidewalk sort of rolling around and walked to Folsom Street, to the bus station not even stopping for a drink.

Well, I had a reason.

I took the bottle of blended whisky out of the bag, undid the cap, and lifted it up to my lips, drinking about a third of it at a go and he said he had never seen a man drink like that. At least I was good for something tried not to remember and started feeling a little bit looser and started talking, not about myself but about things. I took out a smoke and lit it. He asked for one and I knew I had found myself a freeloader.

He lit up his cigarette off mine and I handed him the bottle and he sucked off a swig.

The place was deserted and we didn't pass any cars to the right the hills dripping down eroded could see little caves probably where Indians once hid before the ambush. It would have been a good place to rob me, but the guy looked too soft for that and he'd have had to cut the one-hundred and eighty dollars I had out of my rear before I'd let him have it, us just going up and over hills and past shrubby trees and a tightness behind my eyes starting to set in remembered lifting my head out of the dirt no it was out of a pillow went to the window and looked out. You saw him then, I thought. You saw him and felt him but it doesn't mean you have to carry him around on your back the rest of your life.

Then I took out the terps and undid the cap and drained the whole bottle in one go, because that's the way I worked and also just to make sure it was gone before Elmer got inquisitive.

"What's that?"

"Terps."

"Cough medicine."

"Terpin hydrate and codeine."

"You're sick?"

"You bet I am."

I could feel everything inside of me start to relax and a clarity set in on my mind and I took out the ribs and gave a couple to him and ate the others, throwing the bones out the window as we went I thought if I tried hard enough I could keep it together.

"They're good," he said.

My head bobbed up and down slowly. I didn't like him, but there was no reason I should have let that prejudice me since it would have been hard for me to say what I did like. I looked out the window at the trees. I liked them. They left me alone and the truck swayed along the road. I had taken the bottle back took another slug and then screwed the cap back on and about ten minutes later we came into what was the town.

If I thought the place I had been in before was small and shabby, it was Rome compared to this. A crummy little altar on the side of the road with a crummy little statue and weeds growing around it. There were just about a dozen or so hovels, a few barking dogs and about six vehicles that looked like they hadn't been driven in about five years remembered a long time ago the transmission on my Ford was busted so I dug the transmission of a Chevrolet Club Coupe out of a ditch and welded it in and got it to run for about three months one night ran it off the road. A little store that must have had not much more than some canned goods and candles a small church boarded up. Three unfriendly looking men were staring at us as we drove by and then he stopped at what he said was his aunt's house. It looked like it was made of mud and we got out and went in.

She was a small woman. I don't know if she was pretty or not, but she probably was, though she was plain enough and didn't have on any make-up and she didn't wear her clothes well and when she got a little older she'd probably start fading fast if she wasn't fading already. She couldn't have been much over twenty-five and, since Elmer must have been around the same age, I didn't see how she could be his aunt. But it's a damned incestuous world and I thought that it was just possible that she was his aunt.

Elmer did the introductions.

"Ramona. This is——what's your name again, boss?"

I told her.

"Nice name," she said.

"I think so."

She was looking steadily at me her eyebrows sort of level and eyes showing something and it made my lips go dry and I wanted to speak but there wasn't anything to say. Or maybe there was everything to say and I had all the time in the world, but I didn't think so. No, eternity would go by like a flash.

"I need to talk to you for a minute," Elmer told her.

The two went in the back room and started talking in low voices. It wasn't very polite, but I wasn't at a Thursday of some French duchess and if people didn't want to be nice to me, they didn't have to, damned animals had hardened myself a long time to that kind of thing I once won a dance contest I was sixteen but it had been a long time since I danced.

While they were in there I took a look around. It was a pretty miserable place, and if I say that it means it was miserable alright. There was the room I was in with a few chairs and a deal table and a worn out couch with a slightly less worn out Indian blanket over it. On the wall a bad picture of the Virgin Mary and in the corner a big cast iron stove with some wood to one side the only source of heat but it had been a hot day and was going to be a warm night.

I went to the kitchen and it was poor but clean, with another smaller wood stove, and found a cupboard with an assortment of cups and glasses and took one and went back into the living room and sat down on one of the chairs. I poured myself a drink from the bottle, thinking I might as well try to be civilized.

Then they came out and he opened some cans of beer and they drank beer and she asked about me.

"He's good," Elmer said.

"I wasn't talking to you."

"I have a friend in Aswan," I lied. "That's where I'm going."

"This is a detour?"

"I guess."

Then I started talking, started talking because I didn't want to talk, because I knew that the more I said the less they would understand and it was better than being grilled asked all kinds of questions that I didn't want to answer and maybe couldn't answer the more questions asked the more lies told until the lies take on the color of truth if there ever was a truth Elmer finished his beer opened another scrutinized me I didn't talk about the war and I didn't talk about all the things that had happened a long time ago but talked about some poets and how we were giving out free soup it was easy to get into debt I was just travelling seeing the great country bus rides hitchhiking when I could had they ever seen the pyramids but enough about me.

"Is he really your nephew?"

"You don't believe him?"

Then Elmer broke in. Some long story about his father sister brother wife descendants of descendants. His eyes got big as he talked. Isolated out there, no one knew any more who was related to who, probably marrying their mothers and giving birth to their grandmothers.

"You're not from here. You wouldn't understand," he said.

Well, I didn't want to understand.

It had been early in the evening when we had arrived and it was getting dark now and she lit some kerosene lamps and I thought Jesus no electricity living like animals out here like some tent in the desert is this what we fought for.

I laughed out loud and she frowned.

By then I had had a good bit to drink and I knew that she was beautiful and didn't want to look at her, so looked at my glass and shook a cigarette out of the pack and lit it and we talked, not about anything specific, anything that would give me away or anyone else away and I liked Elmer less and her more.

He bummed another cigarette off me, but she didn't smoke.

I asked where the toilet was.

"Outhouse," Elmer said, pointing through the kitchen to the back screen door.

They really were animals I thought and rose to my

feet and headed for it as steady as I could then out and into the fresh night looked around couldn't find it and urinated eyes cast up at the sky some infernal upside down exhibition of stars was thinking just go easy just go easy and then I saw it, followed it for a couple of steps some ancient ritual of fire, but I had been told before that I was prone to hallucinations.

I went back inside.

"Find it?"

"Yes."

Ramona was looking at the floor.

"Shouldn't we go?" I said to Elmer.

"Go?"

"North."

"It's too late. It's too late and I'm too drunk."

I could have said that I would drive and I could have driven and he probably could have too didn't know what he was drunk on but she was there and I didn't have anyone waiting for me up north or in any other direction so I put another smoke in my mouth and poured the last of the bottle into my glass like the selfish bastard I was and sat down and drank it not so much wondering about the globe of light as wondering how far I might have to travel to come to the world's end.

Blue Boy Montoya

"Don't worry mother," I said. "Everything will be fine!"

She had told me that I always got into too much trouble the time I rode the pig the time I fought with the rooster hid in the woods behind a tree and laughed and laughed so she finally agreed and I took up my Demon Taming Stick went out of the house and down to the creek I'll catch fish I'll catch fish throw stones run fling mud pick flowers climb into trees. So I walked and picked flowers paintbrushes rubbed colorful rocks talked to birds rabbits on springs big trees and little weeds twisted turned threw myself down picked myself up a bee goes buzz buzz buzz ran jumped skipped to the water's edge it told me to go away its long gurgling voice even the water didn't want me around.

"I'm not going anywhere," I said and sat down. "You can leave if you want to, but I'm staying here."

The water sighed. It was full of fish, good ones, bad ones and I sat with my feet in the water watching them swim by feed on my toes and thought how Mom and Dad would like a nice fish dinner we almost never had fish I helped father pick beans from the garden that we had planted in the spring and were already coming along they grew so fast looked at which one might be best to eat some too skinny others too sad or too small little minnow but there was one long and green like cabbage. So I grabbed one of the bad fish—a big one—and threw it on the bank and it jumped up.

"Stay down," I said and hit it in the side with my Demon Taming Stick bap bap.

"Hey, stop that," it screamed. "Don't you know who I am?"

"You're an ugly fish and I'm going to bring you to Mom and Dad. Mom's going to cook you for dinner tonight. She's going to fry you up."

"You little fool," it said. "I'm not a fish. I'm a dragon. I'm Smooth Stone Dragon."

He was sticking out his chest and holding his head up as high as he could.

"I don't care what you are. We're going to eat you for dinner tonight."

"We'll see about that you little runt!"

He swung his tail at my leg and I hit it aside with my stick. And then the two of us started fighting and I laughed because he was very weak and every time he came toward me snapping his mouth and boxing with his fins I knocked him with my Demon Taming Stick blood and tears started coming from his eyes.

"Okay, okay, don't hit me any more," he screamed, blinking a lot and holding his fins in front of his face.

"I told you I was going to eat you," I said, and clobbered him over the head with my stick and he fell down dead.

I laughed and skipped around the dead fish singing a-tisket a-tasket a green and yellow basket then heard a kind of spurting sound coming from the creek. Another fish like the first was standing there in the water and he was crying.

"My brother, my brother, you hurt my brother."

"This fish?"

"It's Smooth Stone Dragon, my brother!"

I laughed. "I killed him, I killed him and with my eye I saw him die."

"You—you," he sputtered. "I'm—I'm Little River Dragon and I'll—I'll . . ."

"You'll be dinner too," I said. "Your brother's pretty small for a meal for three. So I'm going to clobber your head till it breaks too."

I leaped into the water and hit the fish and he hit me back. He wasn't as strong as the first fish, but he was quicker and stopped trying to hit me and concentrated on me not hitting him.

"You killed my brother," he kept saying and I kept swinging my stick at him until he swam down the creek frightened.

Then I leaped out of the water, took Smooth Stone Dragon by the tail and dragged him through the weeds and flowers all the way home again home again market was done the fish in my dish I caught his blood.

Ibbie Montoya

Maybe I had heard it or maybe it was a dream—I could feel him next to me his elbow in my side. A coyote had got a few of our chickens in the night, made off with one and bit the head off another and Theodore was up before me. He took the shovel and buried one. He loves me but I'm not sure how he loves me, not like a mother or sister and not like a wife—I made coffee and eggs, poured a glass of milk for Blue Boy. Then Theodore got in the truck and left and the boy finished his breakfast and ran outside and I was out there weeding around the beans, before it got too hot.

I cried a little, for no reason, and wiped away the tears with the hem of my dress as I weeded. Maybe I was happy. I can't tell the difference anymore there is just a feeling.

Blue Boy had gone out and hadn't come back. He went out to play but it was hard to keep up with such an energetic child—it was hard for us—hard for us to keep up with our blessing because that's what he was I know—thinking he was probably still down at the creek gazing talking to the minnows—hard to be in a dying town with no children to play with everyone stopped having children and we almost did too because the children usually only come with the love. But there wasn't much of it. The cows had more of it than the people. The beans had more.

The boy could already walk when he came out of me. Everyone said he would be a child difficult to handle and they weren't wrong about that they asked me but why was he blue and I said something about the sky because it was like the sky was in our house when he came the house was full of activity, but I was happy then, there was no mistaking that.

The plants in the garden began to grow better and the sunflowers seemed like they smiled and the beans they grew in thick clusters.

And I smiled. Because when Theodore married me I knew it was not for the love not sure what it was for though I gave him the love I had. I had so much of it to give and I gave it. His mind always on that other older than me and if she was once a beauty she was no longer she had gotten too many of the tricks. I still feel like a girl of fifteen and am surprised every time I see myself in the mirror. No, men never looked at me but there were hardly any men to look, either stabbing each other, shooting each other, dying in ditches from too much drink or too many of the drugs.

I hoped that Blue Boy would grow up clean. I worried about him.

He had asked me if he could go play by the creek and I had at first said no and he had laughed and danced and asked me again so I said fine and he ran outside. I was done weeding around the beans and stood up and went inside and washed my hands and came out and saw him coming. He was carrying it as if he had triumphed over a lion or wolf.

"What do you have there?" I asked him.

"A dragon. He looks sort of like a fish but he told me he was a dragon."

"I see. And what do you want me to do with it?"

"Cook it for dinner."

"I'm not going to cook anything that's not cleaned and gutted," I said and so he went out back and cut it open and cleaned out its guts and scaled it and brought it in the kitchen. I covered it and it sat there. Later Theodore came back and I rubbed it over with flour and fried it and served it with the beans.

"Fish?" he said. "Who brought us fish?"

Blue Boy was laughing and I didn't say anything and he repeated the question.

"Blue Boy caught it," I said.

But he couldn't let it go at that and kept asking questions where did he catch it what kind of fish was it and Blue Boy told him it was the good kind us looking over and seeing that what was on his plate was almost gone already so we started eating what was on ours, Theodore eating not exactly like he was enjoying it, but because it was there on his plate.

"Boney," he said. He ate the beans.

And, yes, it was boney but it was also what our son had caught and I thought he should have been a bit nicer about it.

L 5 Flower

I came out of some universal weeping, some crying and screams and rose tall my hair shooting off in every direction light and clouds wrapping around me putting their ears against my flesh listening to my heart as it thundered my hands going up to the roots of the stars my feet to the emptiness of the earth some mathematic mystery singing broke out everywhere but that was long ago when the rocks still had mouths the sea hissed with steam the sky a fibrous net some cosmic jubilation dazed as I came into being bended this way and sideways muscles covering gorges mountains my chest soaked in something oh it was night laying on the waves of tar or warm fragile nothingness oh it was night.

Now how long have I sat thinking thinking power is nothing in this infinite gulf tearing and spreading me out slumbering in eternal visions and little by little felt the yearning sensed it some astrology slow movement in the dust ignored it sensed it another dry whisper heat clinging to me sweat streaming from my cheeks is that what it was I felt sensed it kind melancholy request and dropped down my gaze eye knowing this gaze eye in one got up from my seat of great greatness stepped part way down thigh rubbing against some wayward cloud leaned over and then reached out my hand some thick black beam and picked it up you brim-filled vessel and drank that ancient lava prepared in sandy caves what was offered dark fruit of Saturn sap what reeling away through the trees it was not a glass of hay and leaping up on a thread of sunshine tumbling down and climbing back up onto the sky day by day on the solar ladder I returned through lovely leaves taking that glass not swelling earth or eating comets gulping down boiled moons which rolled over my teeth and weaving my way away and began to listen to what he asked what he asked what he asked like distant voice of alfalfa or pebbles shimmying down a hillside or some old semen falling flat what he asked why me whose father was chaos and mother eternity forever be stranded on this island of time without death or life or death or life.

"Exist."

"Not exist."

"Exist."

"Exist."

Them laughing off away perpetual neighbors humming bird bat but who was I alone though winds came and lived in my ear daylight drained through my mouth and rivers gurgled up at me please and beauty blushed anger yelled blanket without bones shouting bones without weeds groves of skeletal planets bobbing their skeletal heads hectoring me out of my rest you crew of galaxies each demanding patience a thing I gobbled up long before memory sitting in stillness a stillness coughed out of my chest my lips stretching from vastness to vista but there is friendship for who gives me.

Coughed I called out drummed on ponds kicked over little clouds drunk in haunted knowledge summoning Coyote and also the gurgling Galaxy Club them hopping leaping flying to me smiling jabbering joking some flux of fur and wild grins of beaks I let it be understood that this man serving primordial lava juice should have what he wanted my eyes he should cannot be penurious sometimes birds scratch at my feet but enough of that.

"Give them a child," I said.

The Galaxy Club were leaping leaping clapping and bobbing.

"What's a child?"

"They still make them?"

"Someone's been procreating again!"

"Nothing to spare!"

"To spare."

"We don't like children."

"No, we like to beat them chuck them in deep ditches."

Coyote howled and they looked at him some astonishment and chased him and he jumped over to me some friendly snarl licking.

"Maybe better not to get mixed up in human affairs," he said.

"Give them a child," I said again.

"Well then," he said. "The universe never ends. There are no fetuses here, but there is so much sky. In the west there is a patch that no one even leans against. You could give them a part of that."

"Then give them such a piece such a piece of the sky always floating over there dancing floating," I said, "and when it comes out of her it can be their what is it called son what good is power if I cannot use it what good is power give them a son give them a son some child have pity I was given drink have pity."

The Galaxy Club's lamenting uneasy laughter protesting complaining Coyote agreeing licking agreeing oh how I enjoy the licking that soft warm tongue feathers as some bay of light some heated powder.

And so Coyote bit off the sky's hand pain balling it into a fist bleeding azure granules and in the night he went down and pushed it into her and the man was thankful and left a bottle sitting on a rock and I swallowed it stumbling away sleeping sleeping reverberating I could feel their closets opening thoughts expanding if they understood the tides of grief turning back time just briefly so he did just that taking up the sky hand and early in the morning before light came on the earth planting it in the woman's womb what trouble this child would cause what trouble the sky it bled for a day my sleep is so long my sleep is so long but I hear.

Candelaria Griego

Grandfather was the Hermano Mayor. He died a long time ago. He floated out of the room on his back, floated down to the arroyo and away. No one in the house talked or cried. We laid the table and ate. Only the sound of the soup. The sound of spoons and crockery. His chair was empty. The only flavor the flavor of sadness if it was even that. I tasted it now.

Finally mother spoke. She asked me to hand it to her.

I picked it up and passed it to her. Sprinkling salt on her soup, her lips very tight, her moustache looking very black, though I know it was thin. Then she drank off her soup and pushed her bowl away. I wondered how many nights she had floated through the valley.

"Never have children," she said, "they bring you heartache."

I looked down and finished eating. We cleared the dishes and took them to the kitchen. We heated up water and I washed them and Brunilda dried.

"You can't see him anymore now," she said.

"Who?"

"Your boyfriend. You cannot see him anymore."

And later that night she took me out back where the flowers were growing and told me to eat them. I told her that I did not want to. That I could go away. But I knew that I couldn't. There was nowhere to go. Mother had said I had to eat the flowers.

They were long and white. They shone in the darkness. On my knees I picked them and ate them and they were bitter and I knew that she was right, that I could no longer see him. For his sake more than mine. I stood up and knew that grandfather was there, somewhere in the night and that whatever I had come from would be what I would go to. I could not say I won't. Could only stretch out my arms and grab at the night.

"You can ride it now," I heard Brunilda say.

"Ride?"

"Conway."

"Why?"

"Mother says that you need to do the run. Don't be difficult."

Then she was taking my hand and leading me down to the pen. The moon was full and the sky was clear and it was almost like daylight. The beams of the moon were long and I could touch them. They felt like wood.

She opened the gate and let me in. It was tied up to its stake. She untied it and led it to me, handing me the rope. I looked in its eyes which were like two hatchets. Then I climbed on its back and took it by the horns and we began to do the run.

I felt my hair going backwards. My body was something else. It ran out of the pen and across the field and down to the creek then over that. The moon hung in the sky and I reached for it, but it was still too far away. Only its beams were built around us, thickly. I was a long piece of cloth that kept unrolling.

I felt its ribs with my thighs.

It was angry at me, but it had been grandfather who had killed the other. And yes, we ate it. We ate tulip with red chile.

Grandfather. Sometimes I can still hear him, but I turn away. It is more than time that has turned me old.

Big Water Boss

I live under the water and am the boss of it. Everyone better understand that. I command vast legions—of fish, shrimp, sharks and whales. And the dragons are my people. Don't smile, it's true! We brew up storms, sink boats, terrorize citizens on shore, and can make whole cities collapse if we want to. I'm a patient fellow, but when I get mad you'll know it! I'm not here just to water your lettuce!

Anyhow. Anyhow, where was I?

Oh, yes. The Blue Boy. That little bastard.

I was just relaxing for the evening, drinking a bowl of imperial plankton wine and munching on a few pickled sea vegetables, when a visitor was announced.

"It's Little River Dragon," I was told by my portier.

Well, normally I don't like being disturbed in the evening. Too much business is bad for the nerves. But Little River Dragon was my cousin Mountain Stream Dragon's youngest son, and family is family, so I said that he could be shown in and to take away the imperial plankton wine and bring me a bottle of second degree spirulina two-year-old and a few sea grapes, because I would be damned if I wasted the good stuff on a cousin once removed, especially a child of Mountain Stream Dragon's, because he still owed me fifty pounds of evergreen jade I had loaned him back when birds could swim.

Little River Dragon came hobbling in on his one foot and told me what happened to his brother, Smooth Stone Dragon, and how this Blue Boy had killed him and taken him home and how his mother had cooked him for dinner.

"That evening I peeked through the window and saw the whole thing. They had fried him. It's difficult enough living out there in the desert, trying to keep cool and wet, without this Blue Boy coming and hunting us down for no reason at all."

At first I could hardly believe the story, but then Little River Dragon began lamenting so much that I realized it was true and I became very angry and up above a storm began to hit and waves swept over a few small islands.

"This is intolerable," I said. "That the fishermen have caught all the tuna, depleted our waters of cod and herring is one thing. But now they are starting in on the dragons too! Intolerable!"

"He's not a fisherman. Just a little rascal."

I served Little River Dragon three glasses of the wine, which wasn't nearly as bad as I'd remembered it, had three myself, and called in my adjuncts, Grey Cloud Marshal, Dizzy Mist Dragon, and Knifejaw Azhdahā, and told them about the matter. "An almost near relation of mine, Smooth Stone Dragon, has been eaten—fried and eaten to be precise," I said. "I realize that every life must come to an end, but he was young, only a few hundred years old. It's hard times for dragons all right."

I told them the whole story.

Grey Cloud Marshal stepped forward and, after bowing

slightly, spoke.

"Look," he said, "this little fellow is nothing. He might have been able to beat up one of these country dragons, but give me six or seven good deep sea dwellers and I'll go and knock the life out him."

"He's pretty tough," Little River Dragon whimpered. "And he carries a stick that feels like a two-ton boulder when it lands on you."

I imagined Little River Dragon was exaggerating somewhat. Their father had always been a weakling, and it looked to me that his sons were the same. But, to be on the safe side, I decided to take Grey Cloud Marshal's advice and send an entire contingent.

"Get him and bring him back here and I'll have his brains for supper," I instructed.

I suppose I hadn't lived long enough. I hadn't lived long enough yet to understand that everyone should just mind their own business.

Cleopatra

Couldn't move trying and struggling but the pain became more some screaming mariachi some carnival of blood dogs licking at me nothing I could do chained there to some rock tried to move but I couldn't up against some pyramid tomb get off the bandages some nightmare desert trial. Why don't you help me I was saying repeating but knew that no one could I did it for you so let me go begging but no one to ask about it just trying to get free and hearing the camels coming up against me I could hear them talking you nomads. They were shooting at me and I was shooting back. Stuffed myself behind a dune. Something landed near us and a lot of legs were flying through the air. He felt too much pain to even scream too much of it all to even feel shock just big waves of red spilling over us some sound of a helicopter and that constant rattling. I was breathing hard. They were speaking in some kind of slow Latin and I couldn't understand what they were saying, but I knew it was about me. She was probably telling him to get me out of there. I wouldn't blame her. I didn't like myself, so why should she? I just lay there with my eyes closed.

But then I heard the truck door slam and the engine clack on and it drive off and I looked up and rubbed the sides of my face, four days' worth of whiskers. I didn't feel calm at first but then started to, the place not exactly bright but sun coming in through the window, Ra raising his head above the desert horizon because sometimes you have to see to feel.

I sat up and lit a cigarette and then she came in. I watched her, still not quite sure if she was beautiful or the opposite but then she smiled a little, or it seemed like a smile, and she was beautiful.

"Where did he go?"

"To get food stamps."

"You mean you two actually eat?"

"Well, I do. You should try it sometime."

"Coffee?"

She nodded her head and turned in a way that might have been called graceful if one used words like that and went into the kitchen and I could hear her rattling the pots and pans and I got up and snuck around through the front door around to the side chickens pecking in the yard and then, there in the daylight, could see the outhouse. When I came back in there were some fried eggs and some kind of flatbread on a plate and a cup of coffee.

I sat down and ate. The coffee was nice and strong and the eggs were from the chickens out back so they were good and fresh the yolks a beautiful golden yellow. I mopped up the last of the yolk with the bread and rinsed it down with coffee.

"How do I wash up?"

She didn't answer but just went into the kitchen and poured some hot water into a tin basin and told me to go ahead. The wood stove in there was lit and the room filled with its pleasant warmth. There was the mirror on the counter and she handed me a towel and a plate on which was a bar of soap.

I took off my shirt and washed up as best I could, my face, underarms and chest. I wished I could shave, but didn't have a razor, didn't even have a change of clothes. I thought about asking her for a razor, but didn't. When I went back in the living room she was sitting on the couch with a week-old newspaper and pencil, doing a cross-word puzzle.

"The capital of Cambodia," she said to herself.

"Phnom Pen," I blurted out.

"You're smart," she said.

I didn't reply. I knew I wasn't smart. If I had been smart I wouldn't have been where I was thinking about things that I knew could never be true. She continued doing the crossword puzzle, and most of the information she didn't know, or if she knew it, she pretended like she didn't.

"First woman to go over the Niagara Falls in a barrel," she asked.

I gave the answer, though how I knew was beyond me, secret of the pharaohs. And then she asked me a few more questions and I gave her the answers to those too. I guess it made me feel good, and maybe that's what she wanted to do was to make me feel good and for a moment it seemed like life was real and I forgot the bad dreams I had been galloping along on without saddle or bridle just clinging to the mare's blazing mane hunted. She sat there with the paper and I went out in front and lit a cigarette and watched a dog walk by with its head hung low and then walked a few paces myself and then in front of one of the other houses, which was painted turquoise, spotted an old woman sweeping her porch with a broom and she saw me and stopped sweeping, just stood there looking so I could feel her going inside of me snooping around my brain and heart. Her house had a cow skull hanging from a post and not far from her house was another little miniature building without windows or doors. I didn't say anything and neither did she. She had stopped sweeping and was staring at me. I took another drag of my cigarette and threw it on the ground and turned around and went back to the house.

"You've got nice neighbors," I said to Ramona.

"If you don't like it."

"Am I supposed to like it?"

"This is where I'm from."

"You've never been anywhere else?"

"Not really. Not to live."

"Past the Garden of Eden some taboo fruit to Kearney mind still naked a snarl of hair left untrimmed by dreams of sand that devour me up," I said.

"That's a part of a poem."

"You're damned right it is."

"You are a poet?"

I told her I hadn't written the line and that I wasn't a poet, though I had and at least thought I was and so had Gregory Corso and when I told him it was better than "Howl" he had agreed with me or at least said he agreed with me so high at the time he might have seen the truth.

Later Elmer came back. He seemed stoned as hell

smelled like he had washed his hair with solvents. He carried a bag of groceries. Inside there was beer and steaks.

The steak was thick and tasted good. He had bought T-bones with food stamps.

Ramona Roybal

Serafin used to come over. I didn't love him, but he was there for me. Well, he was there. Maybe not for me, but he was there. Then he was shot coming back from town. Someone sat on a boulder and shot him and then he stopped coming over and other men did but I told them to go away. Patricio Chávez came many times and I told him to go away. He banged on the door late at night. I could have let him in, but didn't like what I saw in his eyes. I didn't tell Elmer to go away but he was my nephew and platonic and I couldn't be alone all the time, though it felt like I was. He was funny but didn't make me laugh.

Brunilda would invite me for coffee. We drank it and talked a little. We talked a little. Candelaria made the coffee, we drank it while she stayed in the kitchen or her bedroom. I knew what they wanted, but no. When I was small they gave me some candy and mother told me not to take it from them any more. They should have had their own daughters.

I wished that Elmer had not brought him. He said he had found him, was always talking about finding things, though the only thing he had ever found were vapors.

"He can take the risk," Elmer said.

"Is it worth it?"

"Sure it's worth it, Ramona. It's easier than robbing a bank. Someone should be spending all that dough instead of it just sitting there. Father told me it was there and I've dreamed about it."

I said no and he talked about a ticket to happiness and things like that. But happiness was something I had never looked for. Something that had never looked for me. We were sixty miles from happiness. Or maybe six hundred or maybe six thousand. He thought it was something you could pick up out of the ground or get another to pick up for you. I tried to explain it, but I talked too slow and he thought too fast or too funny and had been telling me about the generations and how they had stored it away, his eyes growing wide and voice sweet until I almost believed it. Or maybe I did and we went back out and there was a bottle on the table.

The man was very tall, but did not look intelligent or handsome. But I never asked for a handsome man anyhow. Serafin hadn't been handsome, but he had been a man. I still didn't know who shot him. It could have been Rafael or Matias. It could have been Patricio. It could have been anybody.

This one. Probably someone with nowhere to go. Running away from something. The men run, the women wait. We grow old and wait. Just like the Griego sisters. But he turned out to be more intelligent than we thought, despite the drinking, and I thought maybe he was good for something after all, but just kept quiet and watched while he slowly got drunk and his eyes got quiet and Elmer watching us both and it was getting dark outside. I was hungry but didn't feel like cooking supper.

He slept on the couch and Elmer slept on the floor of my bedroom with a blanket. I don't know what he thought Elmer was doing but he wasn't.

The next morning I told Elmer that this was the wrong man, but he insisted. He got in his truck and drove away and I turned back toward the house, in me some piece of sunshine that I couldn't think about or explain and later when he started talking about poetry—well the only poets I had known were the creek and the wind and it was nice to know that some men had beauty.

"Why are you here?" he asked me.

"I have to be."

"No one has to be anything."

I guess I was luring him in without even trying.

Demon Taming Stick

I came into being. Was carved out and came into being.

Butterfly Skin is the one who carved me. And put me in the hands of his son. Lichen Stag.

We tamed the Demon with the Eagle-Talon Nose. Into the forest. Hunted. Slaughtered Acorn Demon. Hemlock Badger. Dandelion Wolf Stagger.

Slaughtered.

Fights and adventures.

Lichen Stag became very old. He set me down. Walked off and died.

Lying there on the ground. Sand, moon. Wind, rain. Coyote came and showed Blue Boy. He told him of me. Blue Boy took me to where he ate his food. His mother called me a dirty stick. His father, he did not care.

Blue Boy wished to tame. Lizard Demon Waiting. He came to bask on the rocks every day. We struck him. We struck him and his tail came off. We struck him. He shook and died.

We struck flowers and they fell. We struck branches and they broke.

Struck the dragon. He died.

Cleopatra

"You take the string and lay it out behind you as you walk."

"You sure I shouldn't use breadcrumbs?"

"What?"

"Never mind."

So it was time to play the clown. Why not? If you can't stand up to things you might as well laugh. Elmer had a fifth and poured us drinks and I swallowed mine and had another. I couldn't understand if the two of them were cracked or just plain dumb or a little of both as is the case with most people, the present party not excluded.

I tied the end of the ball of string to a rock and stood outside behind the outhouse.

The moon was floating about six inches above the horizon. I stood there waiting wondering if Pompey was going to come along and talk to me my fingers almost itching why was she letting me do this probably the same reason she let him do that. Then they came, two lights floating through the trees. I figured they were lanterns or flashlights and just wondered who was carrying them. I followed just like some joker in a fairy tale. They moved slowly and so did I. Going through the jungle you had to walk very quietly and I laid out the string as I followed them. Then, after about a hundred yards, the string ran out me standing there in the dark holding up an end of it shaking my head.

I guess Elmer and Ramona were even less intelligent than I was.

I chuckled.

Well, I would follow them without it, walking through the trees at night like this, the leeches in the Mekong Delta I could almost see her smiling at me back there.

Prawn Dragon Colonel

Five thousand years ago on the shores they used to burn chines of beef to me and mine. Yes, great grandson of Poseidon, it was I, Prawn Dragon Colonel, who saw from the briny deep the story of time march forward, cities collapse, rebuilt, rising up taller and more brutal than before, my kind fried, buttered, served up to the hungry jaws of man. Caught in nets, with no escape, it is difficult to beat the foe and at the base of the ocean the funeral marches have been many, the waving of blue banners and the piping on trumpet shells. I have fathered many millions of sons and as many tears have I shed, adding water to water and salt to salt.

But enough of this sorrow. My life has been a marshal one, wrestling with sharks and beating on the heads of stupid whales. So when Big Water Boss sent a tarpon over to tell me to get to his place, I did not hesitate, but thrust aside my dinner and leapt from my seat.

"Finish your miliolida salad before going out," my delightful concubine said.

She was always trying to get me to eat more, as if a fellow could be judged by how much he ate.

So I ignored her comment and, slipping into my pink armor and taking up my six-inch coral trident, swam as fast as I could to the palace of Big Water Boss.

"He seems a little small," Dizzy Mist Dragon said, nodding in my direction.

I looked over my shoulder, but was still unsure who he was talking about. No one small around there. Did he see someone small? Hmmm.

We set out late at night under the command of Grey Cloud Marshal. In addition to he and myself, there were six in our war party: Dizzy Mist Dragon, Knifejaw Azhdahā, Seven Plum Conger, Double Armored Searobin, Warmouth Taninim, and Four-Tusked Shen. Each of us determined to make short work of the fellow, rescue our honor and show the land-dwellers that they had better think twice before plucking little dragons from their streams.

Little River Dragon was to show us the way.

We swam to the surface and mounted our clouds. Chanting our magical spells we rose up and sped through the air and, in about nine hours, were there. A real crummy place. A lot of rocks with a thin trickle of water running between them.

I rubbed my eyes. The light was awfully bright around there.

"Well, let's get on with it," Grey Cloud Marshal said.

"I could do with a drink first," Seven Plum Conger murmured, scratching his throat with his fin.

"Sure," Dizzy Mist Dragon said. "The place is lined with saloons. Want a shrimp roll while we're at it?"

He thought he was a comedian, but no one laughed.

Yes, we weren't exactly on Deep Wine Avenue. The

ocean was far away. No juice to speak of. The wind was strong and dry. I brushed my whiskers, spat and cursed. The other fellows were in no better state of mind, scratching themselves, blinking, frowning. If Smooth Stone Dragon had been stupid enough to live in a place like this, he deserved to be eaten, it seemed to me.

His brother, Little River Dragon, pouted and showed us the way.

"That's the house right there," he said, pointing. "But be careful of the boy's stick, it's dangerous!"

He then made himself scarce and we moved forward. Grey Cloud Marshal, at the front of our ranks, called out and the rest of us began making noise too, stirring up dust with our tails, giving our lungs a workout.

After about two minutes, the boy came out, naked except for a pair of shorts and in his hand a big stick.

"Listen," Grey Cloud Marshal shouted, "you killed Smooth Stone Dragon, nephew to Big Water Boss. Now you are going to have to come with us, to stand trial in the watery deep. We dragons stand together. So don't resist, or we'll beat the bones out of you."

The insolent fellow laughed. "Dragons? You look like seven fish and a shrimp to me. We ate your brother for supper the other night and tonight we'll eat the rest of you. Mother will fry you up in her pan."

"I'll teach this little boy a lesson," Knifejaw Azhdahā said. "Since he doesn't want to come with us, I'll chop him up into little bits. He's hardly big enough for a proper meal, but his brains might make a good tonic."

He carried a snake halberd with red tassels and wore

white clam-shell armor. He showed his teeth which were long and sharp and licked his lips with a thick, white tongue. Despite the heat, it made me shiver to look at him.

He moved forward, flourished his halberd and began to attack. The two fought for about ten rounds. Knifejaw moved with great rapidity, his muscular body diving and dodging, sliding backward and slipping forward. The boy jumped and skipped, now bringing down his stick, now blocking the halberd. Knifejaw was larger and stronger and it looked as if he had the better of the boy, for the latter began to turn and run. He pursued, his weapon raised high and ready to skewer, but then the boy spun around and hit him on the chest with his stick. Knifejaw flew backward and began rolling on the ground coughing up blood.

"I can take care of this runt," Warmouth Taninim said.

He was dressed in silver scale armor with an iron buccinidae helmet and armed with a shark fang sword. His whiskers bristled with anger.

He jumped forward and lunged at the boy's chin, but the latter ducked. Warmouth's tail stirred up the dust, the boy's feet kicked about the dirt. Warmouth's sword whistled through the air. Blue Boy's stick sounded like a hawk swooping at its prey. Warmouth began to pant. Blue Boy grinned.

Then the boy whipped the side of Warmouth's head with his stick and the good dragon fell, blood flowing fast from his mouth and nose.

The story goes on in pretty much the same way. The other five with me got the same treatment. Of those seven, four were killed and three badly beaten. I am convinced that I myself could have taken him and was indeed about to leap forward and show him what fighting was all about when it suddenly occurred to me that it might be best to report back to Big Water Boss before I made a move and so began to run—I mean slowly walk away.

The next day funerals were held for Dizzy Mist Dragon, Knifejaw Azhdahā, Seven Plum Conger and Warmouth Taninim, though the enemy had their bodies. Grey Cloud Marshal and Four-Tusked Shen could not leave their beds. Myself, Double Armored Searobin and a fellow named Dragon Long Tongue were sent to the big brass to deal with the matter.

Matias Armijo

There weren't many of us left. Serafin had been shot coming into town two years before. Someone had sat on a boulder and shot him as he drove by.

Hijole.

That same winter Julian was found dead in a ditch. Drank a little too much and froze to death and when we carried him to the cemetery and buried him the sky opened up and we all saw his spirit go straight up a beautiful thing.

Jimmy was knifed in back of his house. I know because I did that. He stood there and didn't say a word as I drove the blade into his throat. Then he lifted up his hands and grabbed my arm. The knife was deep in his neck and I prayed to the Virgin when I withdrew it. The next day I left a pack of Lucky's for her to wipe away my sin. His funeral was also a beautiful thing and I cried more than anyone.

So messy. Hijole. So messy.

At the funeral the old women had come and stood there. Dry like rocks. Their grandfather had been the Hermano Mayor. For probably a hundred years he had been. They say when he was young he had whipped himself so hard that rain came. They also say he used to smoke a pipe with the devil and tell him to leave the Brothers alone. Then later he lay on his back and floated away. That was before my time.

It was probably greener then. Because the rain never comes for me. I don't have the fortitude.

The Supreme Elder Councilor killed himself five years ago. And Bisente de Jesús Lucero, the Supreme Councilor, is serving a life stretch for having shot a guy down south.

Times are hard. And it is hard to be prudent. I don't know who will carry on the traditions, but we're trying. I'm the warden, Rafael's the treasurer, and Patricio is Supreme Advisor.

We stood by the morada. Rafael had a bottle of La Cofradia. Patricio had a leño. We drank the bottle and smoked the leño some rag weed my eyes watered and I started to cry as I coughed. The sky was turning from blue to red.

It was leaning against the side of the morada and now and again each of us would look at it and now and again each of us would lift the bottle to his lips.

"It'll be dark soon," Patricio said.

"I guess so."

"He died for our sins."

"The land."

"They're registering his blood if we have to give some of ours we have to do it."

"Those old women."

"Someday we'll get the land grant back. Clean this place up. Get the poison out. Sea por Dios."

"It's almost dark."

"You have to keep paying the dues."

"When we get the land grant back we clean it up. Sea por Dios."

Then it got dark. We sat down and waited. No one spoke. Just the stars. I lit a Lucky and handed the pack to Patricio and he took one and handed the pack to Rafael and Rafael handed it back to me, after taking one himself. Patricio lit his cigarette off mine and Rafael lit his cigarette off Patricio's.

We smoked and waited.

Contrafraternity. At one time we filled the morada. Men sitting on both sides. The floor running with our blood. Thinking of this I felt sad. But we were doing our best.

When the time came we got up.

Patricio went and muscled it onto his shoulder. He went first. Rafael picked up the hammer and nails and followed him and I followed Rafael. Calvary. It was a little cool, but I was sweating. Mother of God I was sweating. One of us would get the honor. My palms were sweating. I didn't want it to be me, but I hoped it would be me the old ladies. But if Patricio were carrying it, it would be him. Someone threw a rock through their windows two years before and I helped put in a new one.

Candelaria made me coffee and I drank it. No one said a word while I drank it. Then they gave me three dollars and I got up and left.

We went to Calvary.

"I'll carry it now," Rafael said.

"No."

"I'll carry it."

Patricio let Rafael take it and Patricio took the hammer and nails. So maybe it would be Rafael.

We walked. It was heavy. Rafael was dragging it.

"Take it."

"What?"

He was pushing it onto me. It was heavy as hell. I felt like it was driving me into the earth. Just carry it for a while and give it up. Just carry it for a while and be prudent. So heavy. Hijole.

Patricio took it from me.

The hole was still there when we arrived. We laid it by the hole. We got there, sat down and waited. I could hear Rafael breathing next to me. He sounded like a panting dog from the walk up the hill.

Patricio went to the madero and kneeled near it. He was praying.

I wanted to smoke a Lucky, but didn't dare. I wiped the palms of my hands on my pants. Patricio was praying. They'd choose him. Of course. He would be the fortunate one. Rafael was next to me. It seemed like he was shaking and I might have been shaking too.

I remembered when Patricio had done the penance of the rice. Fifteen or twenty Coke bottles and beer bottles he had crushed. He kneeled on them all day and all night.

Then they came. Like two lanterns. The two sisters their grandfather had been the Hermano Mayor. He was floating out there somewhere. I should have asked them for five dollars for all that work.

They would decide. We got to our feet. I took a step back to be less obvious. To be prudent. Patricio took a step forward, to be more obvious. He said he was ready.

Then I heard it.

There was a sound. Someone was in the dark watching us. The old man would be floating. It wasn't him.

Falling to my knees, but not to pray. Then I crawled around. Quietly I crawled around.

I could see him. The outline of a man. He was big. I could stab him but better not because I didn't know who he was.

I felt for a rock. A big one that was round. And stood up. Moving up behind him, slowly, silently. He did not hear me and I lifted the rock and hit him prudently on the back of the head. He fell down.

I called out to the others. Patricio came and we dragged him in front of the madero.

"Is he dead?" Rafael asked.

"No, but let's kill him."

Then she made a humming sound. It was Candelaria.

"No. You need to nail me," Patricio said. "I deserve it."

She said that it would not be. I'm the warden, and would listen to her. We were going to do it to the stranger.

Rafael and I laid him on the madero.

Patricio was angry. I could feel it coming from him but he drove the nails in with strong blows.

Hijolc.

Cleopatra

I couldn't remember where I had come from not so far back as that some other world of tall things fast-moving shadows long ago under big floating trees the soft smell of eucalyptus wild fennel that had been pissed on puked on some hill of needles and false laughter the river running near boatmen shouting birds soaring. The fennel. They were trying to tell me something but I didn't want to listen and go out into the cold because it was warm in there and I didn't want to go out and then starting to remember some summer long ago crawling through the grass through the flowers some happiness that probably had never been but outside it was cold. I could feel the pain. It was strong in my hands tried to open and close them but don't think I could just some fantastic light in my eyes suspended and knew without even looking that blood was running from my hands.

Then I opened my eyes.

It was morning. The early light of morning.

One nail was through my right hand and another through my left. In the air. I would have said something but there was nothing to say and no one to say it to and I thought that maybe this was the meaning of reincarnation. Just never stop suffering, from one thing to the next. First the asps, then the gunfire.

I would have tried to pull away, but was afraid that I would pull my hand right off. Couldn't exactly call me great one then should have stayed back in Alexandria and let the camels fall where they might I drooled out the words no control was a smile that cannot make head or mouth and you believe it's slower than stone some eternal pickling.

My eyes closed. I was there and thought maybe that is where I should have been. There was some kind of storm and I was cast ashore all the barges lost so that's why I was there but I never even got wet. Crawled out of her womb. Scotty telling her she should never have had a kid with someone like that his thick accent spilling all over the house like a bottle of Famous Grouse.

Then I looked down and he was there. He must have been seven or eight. Maybe nine. Maybe six. Staring up at me with his big eyes, innocent as a child's should be, his skin some peculiar shade of blue. I thought maybe I was hallucinating, but I wasn't.

"Did they nail you up there?" he asked.

I acknowledged the truth of this with a nod of my head.

"Do you want me to get you down?"

I didn't really know how he could do it, but told him that I would appreciate it if he could and he did, though I don't know how. He was a much stronger boy than I had thought he could be.

"Does it hurt?"

I told him it did. I was sitting in the dirt. My hands hurt like hell. I took off my shirt and then my undershirt, and ripped up the latter and wrapped the rags around my hands and then put back on the former.

"I need to get out of this place," I said.

"Why?"

"I guess because after being pinned up like that I don't consider myself to be all that welcome."

"Why did they pin you up?"

"I guess because I was nosing around in their business and they didn't like it."

"You were looking for the treasure?"

"I don't know what I was looking for, but you can see what I found."

"I'll show you where it is."

"Sure you will kid. You'll show me the end of the rainbow and where the leprechauns dance and maybe after that we can sprout wings and fly around a little."

He didn't laugh, but I couldn't blame him. My cornball didn't even amuse me. It wasn't hard to see why I was wandering around like a hunted animal without home or friends. I asked him which way the road was and he pointed down the hill and then went away himself humming some child's tune.

Alfonso Torcuato Southerland-Hevia y Miranda

I am six foot four, slim and of sturdy build. I was born to a poor yet noble family, descended from Spanish grandees who had mixed their blood with the cream of English nobility.

But, though some had prospered, we were indeed the deprived branch of the family.

Father worked the live-long day, picking oranges, driving trucks, cleaning toilets in order to bring food to mother, and I—and my *brother*. He was not my real brother, but had been left on our doorstep by a stranger. Yet I, being of generous and compassionate mind, never complained and swore I would try and love him as one of our own. Probably he had been left by some wayward creature of easy virtue or some poor woman who had been violated by an escaped convict. Because my real family were tough to the core—a people of leather, steel and high learning. There was nothing soft about us, but our hearts, and the only thing we were ignorant of was, um, dishonesty. We had come to this country and built it from the ground up, had made it great, watering the crops with our sweat and, um . . .

Yes, um, brother and me.

Mother always treated him with especial kindness, as

did I, though I was rebuffed often enough and treated like a cad. She breast-fed him until the age of twelve, which was probably a mistake. Father went off to war and was shot through the brain. They buried him under an American flag on an island somewhere in the Sulu Sea. I kept his dozen or so medals in a cigar box by my bedside.

The education I received was by my own hand. I read vagariously but deeply and decided early on that I would do great things in life. If I have not fulfilled my ambition, it is by no fault of my own, for work I have never tired of, toiling away by candle-light and waking many hours before dawn to resume my activities.

My adopted brother—let us call him Todd—is a chemist by profession. I have never heard him called a good chemist, but he has persisted in his work, and for that I give him credit, though it was mother who, by denying me my fair inheritance, put him through school and bought him his shop. He has only poisoned four or five people by accident thus far in his career, and they were people of no consequence, so the world should not treat him over harshly, despite his, um, peculiarities.

I will not go into those because I was sworn to secrecy and because I plan to keep this thing decent, so even children can read it. Though, properly speaking, I never had a childhood myself.

It was another day in paradise, one of brilliant sunshine. A soft, warm breeze blew in from the south, carrying with it the smell of the distant sea and I could imagine myself running along the sand—then me and my lady love gripping each other in an impassioned embrace as a thousand sea-gulls circled overhead, her purring into my ear like a kitten.

Of course I had no lady-love—or, um, should I say many—yes, so many that the choice was a difficult one. My Spanish blood provided me with ample ability and being so handsome, I had to keep the women at bay with a large stainless steel rod.

I sighed.

I fired up a Winston and headed to his establishment to bring him some baked goods. I thought maybe we could drink a cup of tea together and discuss his future prospects. I pulled up in front of the place, slid the gear shift into park and got out of the Cadillac Coupe de Ville. The curtains, which were some striped jute affair, were drawn and the sign on the door read closed.

His car was there so he must have been also. He did not walk, as a habit or otherwise. I frowned. Mother had given him three thousand dollars to set himself up in business. She had known that, without help, he never would have survived. She was a woman of high charity.

I knocked lightly on the door, and then entered, bowing slightly as I did so. His face was rather red, as if he had been slapped numerous times. I asked him if this was in fact the case and he agreed. He was, understandably, embarrassed.

I laid my hand gently on his shoulder and told him how fond I was of him. Sometimes it is better to lie than speak the truth. I asked him if there was any way I could help, but of course he was unable to appreciate this offer of assistance, because of the ungrateful streak that ran through him.

"Is it another woman problem?" I asked him gently.

"Yes, Alfonso," he admitted in a pathetic voice. "She came in and toyed with my heart."

"And slapped you."

"Yes, I tried to kiss her and she slapped me."

"You were only trying to kiss her?"

"Well . . ." He grimaced.

I understood. Women would not have him voluntarily, so he tried to take them by force. An ugly habit.

In a shrill voice he explained the situation. He had tried to take advantage of her and, in the end, she had taken advantage of him.

"Her name?"

He hung his head and told me.

I bought a pack of gum from him for ten cents, told him to leave things to me, and walked out the door. I slid behind the wheel of my car, started the engine and got out of there.

The light in the boulevard turned amber. I slowed my vehicle to a halt and lighted a cigarette. I would take care of the problem, but the first order of business was getting something to eat.

I stopped at a little place I knew on Central Street. The maître d' showed me to the best table, which was in a corner near a window draped with persimmon-colored curtains. I ordered a bottle of Bordeaux and a fillet mignon. The food was, as usual, splendid and I ate with a hearty appetite. For dessert I had an éclair and a cup of strong, black coffee.

"The check please, Jean Pierre," I said when I was done.

"Please, Mr. Torcuato Southerland-Hevia y Miranda, it

is on the house."

I tried to slip him a twenty dollar bill as tip.

"No, no. If Monsieur Dumas knew I had taken money from you, who has helped him so often, I would lose my job."

I hated leaving without paying but did not want to insult Jean Pierre. There were tears in his eyes as he saw me go. He was the best waiter in town and I would be there for him when he needed me. And, eventually, he would need me.

I got in my Cadillac and headed north, into the green foothills.

Theodore Montoya

If I was going to paint it, I'd paint it blue. The pink I had put on more than thirty years ago, just before she came there, had gotten pretty dull. And Ibbie likes the color blue. It was our boy that came out of her. Probably four or five gallons would be enough. Latex. An afternoon's work, or maybe two. I've never been shy of a little work. Up before everyone else. The livestock. The garden.

When I was a boy. Seven. We had come down from the north and squatted, with a horse and three sheep. There were more people here then, but even with more people, not many. Perhaps four hundred. About fifty of them worked in the mica mines, which were still open, though already it was a commodity not much in use. But my father wanted land and there was land, pretty good grazing land, so he took it. Uprooted trees, built a house, gave us a life.

The location was fine.

The three sheep turned into five, and the five into twelve and I would tend to them take them to the creek to drink let them eat the green grass. Watch them grow strong and almost fat. We killed one and ate part of it and gave meat to the neighbors and sold the rest in town and mother fried the fat, the best food I had ever had and when winter came snow blew over us.

Later we changed from sheep to cows and the town changed.

But every place has its problems.

I drove by and saw her, back turned toward me but I could well imagine her face, had seen it so many times thought about it so many times more, at first with desire, then with regret, and finally with reluctance, pressing down on the clutch shifting into third gear pressing on the gas before she turned cast on me her eyes swinging around the bend past the graveyard and out of sight I looked at her through the mirror until the end.

She had once been something rare and soft. Beautiful. Perhaps ten years older than me. Her breasts sang honey. Features majestic some queen that I might have been told of in childhood slept for and worked for while the grass waved its arms I remember her taking me in her arms. Yes, she took me. She reached for me. I spoke her name and almost fell against her. Me kneeling at her feet, burying my head in her stomach some knight of the House of Montoya. I knew what they said and perhaps even knew that it was true grandfather, mother, sister, but at the time it was easy to forget. My eyes were closed. She ran her hand through my hair put it under my chin a kind of benediction. I opened my eyes and looked up at her feeling my mind at once go still and racing forward on hope. That was a long time ago.

Hope.

Well, maybe it never entirely dies.

She would walk to the orchard and meet me. She never talked much, but by her eyes I thought I knew how she felt, and I spoke to her as softly as I could.

"We could get married," I had said. But she answered that she would never get married. Perhaps could never get married.

She said it without feeling, but she must have felt something. Certainly she must have.

And I thought but never talked and then one day she stopped going there. I waited. For about two years I waited. Walking there alone, staying alone, walking home alone. And when I saw her she looked at me and looked right through me. It was then I knew that she had nothing more to give me, not even words.

How many years did it take?

Ten to find a woman ten years younger than me and another twenty before the words came out.

"I'm barren."

I had heard the word before. Used for places where the dirt was red or too sandy or too rocky and nothing would grow.

"Barren?"

"I think so. Why else?"

And I thought for a long time about grandfathers before grandfathers and also her and that I had never given her much, I couldn't, but that she should have that if nothing else and then I started laying things down, at first just an apple and then a few cobs of corn or flowers and day after day I did that laying it down on the rock by the field and inside asking for it not rationalizing but knowing that seeds fall down to earth some grow into cabbages some into trees or mountains or fast rushing rivers even if they don't culminate from love.

I laid it out but nothing came. I thought of Our Lady and putting it there but I wouldn't. The rock in the field. I put the whisky there. Every day I put it there. First a glass and then another. And then the glass and the bottle.

Who did it and why?

Yes, I had eaten a bit of the first fish, boney as it had been, but when he showed me the others lying in the yard I'd thrown them in the compost. He had to learn to stop killing things needlessly.

Going around the bend and passing the building that had been boarded up, falling down since then and he was there walking along the side of the road. The same one I had picked up a couple of days before. He wasn't hitchhiking now. Just walking. His head hung down and sorrow showing in his steps and he had rags wrapped around his hands.

Perhaps they had done it again. Perhaps she had done it again. Yes, it did not frighten me but I always wondered what might have been. I had stayed away from the Brotherhood, maybe that was why but it wasn't them who gave us a child.

I slowed down and motioned to him and he climbed into the cab of the truck.

"Going into town?" I asked.

"I guess so."

I let there be silence just the sound of the engine sound of the road sound of me switching gears though I could hear him also. Hear the pain of a man, because I too had felt such things for a long time and then without looking at his hands decided to speak.

"Did you ever find that work?"

"I guess I did."

Who knows why I asked a question that would just cause sorrow, the last thing I intended to cause since work was the last thing anyone could ever find there. Men who lived on food stamps dreams revenge hate and spirit. The only fresh things were in my garden, or maybe Ramona's eggs, but the sisters no longer even had chickens, just the goat, the very old goat.

"By the way, my name's Theodore Montoya."

"Mine's Cleopatra."

"Nice to meet you, Cleopatra. You have a last name?"

"I don't think so."

No, he wouldn't. The last name. Only humans had it, and for all I knew he wasn't human or was but some other kind.

"You hurt yourself."

"I fell down."

"Yes. People have been falling down for years in our town. They used to send them from the Church, and they fell down. Then they sent people from the Census Bureau, and they fell down. And now you."

"And you?"

"I also fell down. But I got back up."

"That's what I'm trying to do."

"You have to."

We got to town. I told him he should get something for his hands. After I dropped him off on the corner, I went to the hardware store. I bought five gallons of blue paint, then a few rollers and a small brush for the trim.

"What are you going to paint?" she asked at the counter.

"My house."

"Well, if you ever get tired of doing that, come and paint mine."

I smiled, because one had to be polite.

Elmer Roybal

I know what they had just as everyone knows yes we are all scared of them who knows how many they have put in bondage hurt and pinned down in any case my plan is sound or I think. Had been asked to help out and remember they said whip yourself so I did scourge yourself so I did. Whatever you say boss. Difficult to be part of the community and afterwards they served hot food but it was a long time before I could lie down in comfort and in other years when the time came close I was somewhere else doing anything else so she says she has been feeling tired a mineral deficiency what kind I ask and she says something about zinc and I say you don't need zinc you need gold they have it and I will get it. But they told me to come one night and I did and then they said never return because the funds were missing I say I didn't take them boss but I did and after I was outside on the ground and they were kicking me but I couldn't feel it because the cement. It was only about four dollars. I couldn't feel it I had breathed two cans but I am talking about the zinc and it was over two days.

"It's a rumor," she says.

"No."

"It's nothing but a rumor."

"No."

I'm looking in her eyes now, deep into them trying to go into them show her I'm here in front of her nothing to feel bad about I'm here. And then I explain things to her about long ago and how they had come here already wealthy descendants of Spain them like us carrying whatever treasure they had and then adding to it generation after generation healing pigs and chickens to put away the money that no one else had they could make the crops prosper or wither it was their grandfather who boarded up the church chased the priest away with more cactus riding goats around at night and some pit in the earth full of bills and coins probably in a big chest but am not sure about that part where it is. She's looking at me like she doesn't believe, but she has to, has to.

"I'll fix it," I say. "Don't worry, I'll fix it."

My grandfather had two children twenty years later took to another woman an aunt older than me every time I saw her felt some wonder some crisis going off to some far away place the sea I have never seen the sea. No I have never seen the sea but discovered other things as a kid. When I was born back in the shed I wasn't breathing and so the midwife took me and dropped me in the cistern and I started breathing they say.

Remembering a long time ago maybe I was ten or twelve or fourteen taking the can of glue and holding it up to my nose and breathing, saying that I could hear something in my ears, what was that I hear in my ears. Them saying that was the sound of the ocean, asking me if I could hear the rushing and looking up the sky was bright pink and my face was burning burning hot. I was outside myself looking at myself one big grin.

"They're going to kill him," she says.

Kill him. Well why not isn't it almost the point the problem is I still don't know where the minerals are if I could just dig it out but if someone is going to be killed it isn't going to be me the only way to make money in a land like ours magic and I have tried lighting green candles and I left a cigarette for Our Lady and some Indian paintbrushes but I tell her that this is the surest way I can think of the two of us in a dying town we can go somewhere else she won't even have to change her last name some picture of us walking in the sand by the sea. The sea. We'll send a postcard to the old women. Now she's looking away and we go back out and he's drinking, he's bigger than I am does he see it in her?

And I drink, don't talk much, now remember, when I was even younger, maybe five or six or seven, and the rooster came and jumped up on me and the old man saw it and threw a rock and broke its back, then later there was so much cement and I would take it and the world would become soft not hurt as much. I'm in back of myself looking at myself from the back.

"If there was any money, do you think they would be living here?"

"They don't care about money. Not for what it can buy."

"Rafael and Matias and Patricio."

"They don't know, but the old witches don't care."

"It doesn't make sense."

"I am not saying it makes sense, Ramona. Nothing

makes sense. But I think it's there."

I had seen it in my sleep more than once golden and shining. Now I'm giving him the string and he's grinning and shaking his head and he isn't coming back he really isn't too clever they set up the barber's college and tried to get me to go my hair growing long my father paid for the course and I went once but never went back.

"Maybe he ran off with it," I say.

"I'm worried."

"Don't worry."

"If something happened to him."

"If he ran off with it."

"Something happened to him."

I'm about to touch her hand but she looks at me and gets up and go away lie down on the couch and close your eyes and just wait. Just wait. My eyes are closed and I'm waiting.

Gilbert Trujillo

I was leaning on the counter dreaming. Of everything and nothing. Of the early mornings when I woke up alone, with no company but the dog and the radio. I was dreaming of the flowers that might go with my life—they would be bluebells, or big tall flowers I could climb up, lie on, without any clothes and without shame. Because I have nothing to be ashamed about, not even my tears, which sometimes fall without anyone seeing them.

I was thinking like this and thinking about when I was an infant and all the infants in the world. And the infants who grew up to be men. And the men who grew into other things—whose blood was red and who could stand under a heavy rain with head thrown back beautiful and smoothing down my moustache with my fingers thinking how there was poetry in simple things toys on wheels leaping on a bail of hay and hearts budding with desire and about the childhood of my emotions, their puberty and growth like birds eating seed before winter, a liquor growing mellow, some hand that would be my own to raise to my lips with respect entwine its fingers in my own.

Then the door opened and she walked in.

It was the second time she had come in in three days. I had shivered the first time her well-built muscular figure stretching the confines of her garments and something got a hold of me the second. A hold of me in my chest, in my heart and I probably blushed, behind my smoothed-out moustache I probably blushed and my hands instinctively clutched wishing for some granite-hard shoulders.

"What can I do for you, sir?" I asked.

"Elixir terpin hydrate. Two 4 oz bottles," she replied.

It couldn't have been a better opening if she'd dropped her handkerchief because if you give a favor she just might offer one in return and I knew that was what she wanted and I knew she didn't have a cold—and I also knew that I could have given her many things—of both this world and a higher one—something a lot stronger than that if she were nice to me and if we could both get over our natural timidity did I see a glittering in her eyes?

I smiled.

"Are you new in town?" I said.

"Am I what?"

"New. Before the other day I hadn't seen you and I know just about everyone in town so———"

"If you don't want to sell me the damned stuff just say so."

"Oh, don't get the wrong idea, sir. I want to sell it to you. I really do, sir. But if you wanted something to help your—well, to help your *cold*, it might be better to———"

"You just like to exercise your jaw, do you—take it out for a lap in the morning?"

Well, it wasn't exactly morning. But, yes I did like to exercise my jaw how did you know I thought and knew that she must have had a soft side to her and, after hesitating a moment my hands softly on the counter eyes softly on hers, started talking. At first moving around in circles, without being too direct, and then letting my heart do a little speaking, telling her that it got lonely in there and that people in the town didn't always understand me and it was hard and it was hard really hard and that elixir terpin hydrate (in a 4 oz bottle) was alright but there were things I had in back that would make her feel a lot better—something that would get rid of more than just her cold and——

"I'm not like that," she said.

"Of course you're not! Who is! I was just saying that—"

"I know what you were saying. If you want to let me see what you're talking about."

"Sure, sure. Anything you want, sir. Just about anything you want."

I looked down and saw that her hands were hurt. Poor girl. Maybe she had fallen off her bicycle. Or maybe someone had beat them with a ruler. I was trying to keep my lips flat, but they smiled.

"Do your hands hurt?" I asked.

"No, I just keep them wrapped up like this to keep the dirt off."

I told her I would take care of her. She didn't need to worry, because I would take care of her and her sweet hands and make them feel better. I would make the pain go away and wouldn't let anyone hurt her again.

I went and flipped the open sign to closed, turned the key in the lock. We couldn't have anyone walking in on us. My fingers clenched against my palms a bit moist if people could see me now I thought, nothing to be ashamed about, even if I was crying for her—walking smoothly—keep it calm.

"If you'll just step around over here, ma'am."

"What?"

"Just step back here, señor."

She came back following me as nervous as I was starting to stare around and the boxes and jars touching this one touching that one. Certain situations are very difficult, especially if you are shy.

"First for your hands," I said and took down some Ace bandages and a bottle of hydrogen peroxide and set them on the counter next to me.

"That's not all I want," she said in a husky voice. I could feel myself trembling.

"I know. You've got a little cough. I think I can help you out with that too. I think that I can——"

"Just the terps is all I want," she said.

"That's all you want, honey?"

And then I explained how things were and that it was a pretty lonely town and it would be nice to wake up to more than just the dog and the radio did she like dogs did she like music gave her four bottles of McKesson's elixir of terpin hydrate with codeine and said there would be no need to pay for that because friends trust friends if I just had a girlfriend and then I gave her what I had—smile—hope the moustache looks good—and asked what else I could do for her.

"How 'bout I do something for you?" she said.

I could hardly speak and just stood there, holding my

breath like a little boy. She shouldn't have been using her hands like that. They might get infected. I looked in her eyes and could see a million horizons, a million happy Sundays, could hear a thousand melodies my throat becoming dry and lips opening up like for some quenching drink. But then it came flying into my stomach and all the breath went right out of me and then it flew against my chin. First I went forward and then I went backward.

"Ma'am."

"Who am I?"

"Tell me. Tell me who you are."

"Cleopatra."

"I knew you were. I just knew you were, honey," I said crying now because it wasn't going to work—get on your knees—last chance—and she was leaving. I would probably never see her again—just heartbroken—listen to the door slam.

Vicente Griego

I died long ago but am still here flat on my back. Better to look up at the sky than down at the earth. Don't tell me I'm cursed, because you don't know the meaning of the word. I cursed a lot. Sent curses and sometimes cures. Work is something you're born into, even die into. Living in the spirit world is the same as living anywhere else. No escaping problems. They are everywhere.

Most of the Brothers, when they died, went to various places, but I stayed here. Where my father's father's father came a long time ago. It was he who set up the morada and he who showed everyone Calvary, but now it's just my granddaughters who are left and a few daft young men fit only for penance and hardly fit for that.

Sometimes I whisper to the girls, if they can still be called that. They pretend that they cannot hear me. Who can blame them? A lot of trouble to be tied to someone on the other side. But it could be useful. Learn from those who have gone before you.

There is no evil. No good. No here or there. No use explaining if no one listens. But maybe no use even if they do. Spirit is powerful. Our father Jesus sweated blood and that sorrowful mystery covers everything, from the mesa on down to the creek bottom and up the other side.

A long time ago houses were built. The idea was that if you built houses, more people would come. But when one came, two left. People are scared of old customs. Scared of the hills and scared of the trees and of the sound of their own voices. So they leave.

My wife hung herself. But not before showing our daughter Adelina the ways. Much later, when I stabbed Sergio, my son-in-law, she did not mind. He had not treated her well, but had given her the two girls.

They come, they leave.

When Father Moreno came, he probably thought he could get everyone to be around forever. Put up a wall and open the doors and people will come. I shook my head but remained silent. He had some money and put up the walls and then big vigas were cut down for the roof. We watched from a distance and shook our heads. When we met at night, I told the Brothers not to worry, but also not to offer him any hospitality. When he did open the doors, I don't know what happened. I stood and looked at the building, the dust blowing by it, the wind maybe thinking of blowing it away, like it had done to so many other places.

Everyone believed in the blood of Christ, Our Savior. But this Moreno was an outsider. He didn't understand us. That his god might have had the same name as ours, but was not the same. Later I felt badly and tried to explain, but he refused to listen. Wanted to talk, but not listen and his smile was not a smile but just something painted there and his ears were like they were made of wood. Then one day I came home and he was talking to Adelina. She had offered him coffee and he was there drinking it. Sitting in our house. And he continued to come and she, during that period, stopped floating through the valley.

She was forgetting what her mother had taught her.

At the morada I told them not to worry. That I'd take care of it. The Brothers agreed that it had to be taken care of. Moreno had been busy, telling our daughters and wives and sisters that our way was not the true way of the Lord.

Then came Good Friday. It was morning. I stood there and watched. She came out of the house, dragging the girls, walked down to his church and went in. A dozen women must have gone there.

Did she want my granddaughters to become daft?

So I went and got a hammer and nails and some old barbed wire from a fence repair and my machete and wheeled the wheelbarrow up on the hill in back of the house. The chollas said that I could cut them down so I chopped off their arms and filled up the wheelbarrow with them, placing them in carefully, two by two.

I wheeled the barrow up to Calvary and then walked down to Flores Lucero's house.

"Get Ezequiel and Manuel and the rest of the boys and see me at the bottom of the hill, to Calvary," I told him.

I then went to the church. The service was over. Moreno came to me when I walked in.

"Father Moreno, I want to show you something," I said.

"What is it?"

"It's important that you follow me."

"It's important that you follow the true way of Jesus Christ," he said.

I nodded my head in agreement and he followed me toward Calvary. He didn't know the way. He had never been there before. We stopped at the foot of the hill. He spoke much about what the truth was, but knew little of it. Knew nothing of the path of Our Lord, Jesus of Nazarene and the suffering he had been through, and when we got there I looked in his eyes and saw fear like two beetles looking for a place to hide.

I asked him if he wanted to learn something about religion and finally get some grace. He did not answer, but the sky did. We were giving him a privilege.

He turned around and saw the Brothers step out of the piñons. Eight were empty handed. Two carried the madero. Ezequiel carried the flute. Father Moreno's smile was very exaggerated.

The Brothers held him. They stripped him to the waist and held him. I fashioned a crown out of the cactus and then tied some more to the end of a stick along with some barbed wire. Then put the crown of cholla around his head and started to flog him with the other. The brothers still held him, silently. He pulled but they still held him. He pulled very strongly.

Then the madero was placed on his shoulder and he almost collapsed. He had never held anything heavier than a wafer, had never dug the ground or slaughtered a cow. He was weak.

I told him to move on and he asked where and I told him I was taking him to Calvary. I flogged him with the cholla rod as he went. The rod of cactus and barbed wire. This was the true meaning, of Golgotha, of the Mystery.

It took us a while to get there, but that was good. The flute was played and we sang. I told him to keep his hands still otherwise it would hurt more. His fingers were struggling.

I was doing him a favor only he didn't realize it. Not vindictive. If I had been I would have filled him with worms or made him go blind.

The next day he was no longer in our town.

Then I took a hammer and nails, the same hammer I had used the day before, and boarded up the church. Adelina started floating through the valley again and I was pleased for this. Pleased also for the girls.

Sometimes I talk to the pines and tell them these stories. But even they don't like to listen. Neighbors. They are always like that. Even the goat just shakes its head. It is probably still angry at me for Tulip.

Floating through the pine trees I went down to see. The girls were there and he was following them at a distance, laying out the string behind him. I would have laughed, but did not have the ability. If I tried it was like a thick mist.

He was carrying the string and also a heavy load.

And then he ran out of the string and stood there. He didn't know what to do. He should have turned around. But he didn't. His load was so heavy. He kept following the girls straight toward Calvary. The earth was still wet from the priest and damp from the many others and before that I had gone up and had the honor to spill my blood. I felt like telling him to go back. But if he had come that far, why not let him go the rest of the way? If he wanted to learn about traditions, let him. There is nothing wrong with that.

The three who called themselves Brothers were waiting up there. I had seen them go. No flute, no songs. Times have changed. No matter how much I whisper.

A long time ago it was my father who boarded up the Devil. He had been causing trouble, mostly with the animals, and sometimes with the women. So he threw him a chicken right by our house. And while he was eating the chicken, boarded him up. Like I had boarded up the church. So the Devil isn't free and Father Moreno is gone, but there are still bad little things.

Times have changed. The traditions are ghosts. And so looking up at the stars I floated away.

Rafael Crisantos Baca

When I did the inventory there were two blindfolds. One with a hole, one without. When I did the inventory there was the crucifix on the wall, value ask my heart. When I did the inventory there were six coils of rope, two benches and three chairs. When I did the inventory there was the rule book, bound with a rubber band. When I did the inventory there were some hymns. Hand written. The old songs. When I did the inventory there was a flute, but it was cracked. Outside I did the inventory. There was one madero. Weight: heavy. When I did the inventory there was $5.32. In change. So I went out and got a bottle of La Cofradia and gave Patricio $1 to get a leño from his cousin. After paying off these expenses, there remained 27¢. In change.

It should be noted that I, Rafael Crisantos Baca (Treasurer), and Patricio Chávez (Supreme Advisor) had paid our dues, but Matias hadn't. May the real Jesus who we preserve deliver us from evil, even Matias.

Coyote Ferox

I had told him from the beginning, but of course who ever listens to me—not that my intelligence isn't regarded, but that it is always looked on with suspicion, as if the only reason I would gaze at the night was out of self interest.

A long time ago things were simpler. I showed the people how to play together and how to sing together. I would only eat grasshoppers and got along with everyone and everyone got along with me. But then the moon started playing his tricks and the sun joined in. Time passed. The people found out how to kill. Some bones were there that I ate. Their screams and anger. They lost their trust in me. I showed my teeth and snapped at their legs.

They said that I was fierce.

I would live in one place and then another, but always moved on. There were hot days when I had nothing to drink and lay down exhausted, my tongue hanging out.

I looked but never found the world's end.

So for many years I've stayed here, more out of laziness than anything else.

If the humans see me they shoot at me, try to poison me, trap me, because I drink the blood of their chickens, bite their sheep and sometimes bleed their calves and would not mind biting one or two of them if I could—

feeling a certain amount of betrayal. I helped them, I did. And now. Treating me like garbage. If they would just leave me a few morsels of meat it would be fine. But the world becomes not so easy to live in, having to dance across the road with great velocity lest my corpse be left on the pavement to their undoubted giggles—pin me up on some post they would—not that the creatures of the water are much better. With their constant lamenting persecution complex, though their territories are vast and rather untouched compared to mine, fenced off on every side and so forth. Hard to move. Yes, the earth is closed in by roads and even the sky is now populated by fools.

Fools in the sky, fools on the earth, and the water has its share too.

When I heard the noise I opened my eyes and went to see.

Three fishy types were there jabbering at the old boy. I went and sniffed around. They smelled like snakes and then one pushed me away and said I shouldn't sniff at a dragon.

They were causing a commotion asking L 5 Flower to help them do away with the Blue Boy. Something about him hurting a cousin once or twice removed from someone. They were a delegation sent up to talk to him—aggressive bowing, obsequious chest-thumping, dripping here and dripping there—and L 5 Flower, bless him, was rather bewildered I suspect. His cloudy house had never heard so much noise.

One who called himself Dragon Long Tongue was speaking:

"He is unruly and disrespectful and, to be frank, you were somewhat irresponsible to put him on the earth. If we creatures of the sea and sky are to get along, you are going to have to resolve this issue!"

Fish talk in a funny way and I laughed and offered my opinion saying that I thought they were exaggerating.

"He simply took a minnow from the river," I said, "and would have done nothing more if you had not, in a fit of overreaction, sent your soldiers out to apprehend him—a little boy. Let's forget the whole thing, have a few cups of wine together and beat on some drums."

A fellow with a fat lip, who looked like he had received a good beating himself, bridled. "It was not a minnow! Not a minnow at all! He was Smooth Stone Dragon, nephew to Big Water Boss. You think we've come here to drink wine and dance around to the sound of your miserable drums? Here you are perched on one dismal squirt of a cloud, but it's us who send the real rains. If our boss let's us that is. And you can be damned sure he won't send any rains as long as that Blue Boy is down there rifling through the rivers and creeks for dragons!"

The water folks were not easy to get along with. I showed my teeth. The Galaxy Club were there laughing, but that was nothing new. They are always around if there is trouble and always laughing.

Now things might have quieted down eventually if just then another type hadn't burst in on the scene. We might have told the fishy dragons that we would reprimand Blue Boy and have left it at that. But that's not how things happened.

She was missing one arm and, in the crook of her other, was carrying her own head. In a shrill voice she started crying out about the Blue Boy too.

"He beat me, unprompted he beat me. Yes, instead of sending some nice young man down to earth who might suffer for the sins of others, you sent down a little beast. A little beast who can laugh while terrorizing a woman, a maiden!"

I felt like nipping at her, but I couldn't.

The problem with her was that she was rather well connected and though on earth the people had mostly forgot about the rest of us, they still thought something of her. People somehow made a big deal of this lady and her sisters. I imagine it is because she looked like them, while the rest of us didn't.

Hearing all these complaints L 5 Flower let out a sigh and scratched himself. Apparently dust can even collect on clouds.

"We'll go and chop him up for you," the Galaxy Club volunteered.

"Let them do it," the dragons said in unison.

"The boy has never repented," Our Little Lady of the Trunk added. "He should be chopped up and thrown in a bottomless pit."

L 5 Flower let out the longest of sighs.

"It was Coyote Ferox licking Ferox who suggested I let him be born," he said. "He can go and eat him. He has always wanted to bite a human is the boy human let him bite him."

Well, no. The Blue Boy wasn't precisely human. But I

said that I would do it, thinking that maybe I could think of some way to save him. Then I jumped down to earth to look for him. It took me about an hour to find him. He was playing in the dirt not far from the goat pen, scratching around in it with the lady's arm.

He liked it there, but he couldn't stay. Everyone would see him and then we'd both be in trouble. I explained this to him.

"You've caused a lot of mischief," I said. "Now they want me to eat you. And if I don't, the Galaxy Club will come looking for you."

"They can't hurt me," he said. "I've got my Demon Taming Stick. I'm not afraid."

"Well, you should be. If it comes out that I'm deceiving, they'll not only chop you up but probably your mother and father too. And that stick might work against fish or dragons or plaster virgins, but it won't do much good against the Galaxy Club. They like to be hurt. They actually enjoy it and, instead of obeying the laws of cause and effect, they live in the world of effect and cause."

He looked down at the ground, pouting.

I told him that we would figure something out. That he should let me just take a bite of his scalp. "Then I'll take it back and they'll think I ate you," I said.

"But look how skinny you are," he said, pointing at my belly. "No one would believe that you just ate me."

It was true. Times had been hard. I had dined on a couple of their chickens a few days before, or a chicken and a head to be precise, but hadn't eaten anything since then and my stomach was empty. Some dinner would have been nice.

I looked around for something to eat instead of the boy. The only thing in sight was the old goat, Conway, over in the pen. He would have to do.

We went over to the pen. I untied him and opened my mouth wide, first putting it around its head, working it back in my throat so I could feel his horns poke against it as they went down. He was so tired he hardly noticed as I ate him, though his hind legs kicked a little as they disappeared. I had eaten goats before, but none like that one, some bad rough taste that was hard to keep down. He moved a little, slowly, in my belly. But in any case, now I looked fat.

"Do you think they'll believe you?"

"Almost," I said, "but come closer."

He did and I snapped up a piece of his scalp with my jaws.

"Ouch!"

"Now you had better keep out of sight," I told the Blue Boy. "If anyone sees you . . ."

Thirty minutes later I was back up with L 5 Flower. I felt heavy and a little tired. He asked me about the boy.

"I ate him," I said and held up the bit of blue scalp.

The Galaxy Club grabbed it from my paw and tossed it between them.

"It looks like a piece of his scalp," one of them said, "but that doesn't prove that you ate him—a tricky coyote like you."

I stuck forward my belly. "What do you think is in here?" I said tapping it. "I haven't eaten so well in years."

One of them rubbed my belly. Another kissed it. A third was chewing on the scalp. They all began to run backward in a circle crying out that this was an occasion for celebration. Sun Hair rolled out a big jar.

"This star wine has been fermenting for about two thousand years. It's still a little young, but if you don't mind . . ."

The Galaxy Club had never been nice to me, but if they wanted to start, why should I mind? I nodded my head and they poured me a cup.

The liquor was fabulously sweet and I licked my lips after drinking it. They laughed and poured me some more and I drank it warming my mouth and throat tingling my paw. Then another cup and my head felt light. It was getting hold of me.

They kept filling my cup and I kept drinking, them slapping me on the back and singing maybe they were better than I thought, hard not to laugh, my lips curled back.

Then one of them took my jaws and held them open. The others lifted the jar and started pouring the wine right down my throat, it going down, spilling out, me getting wet with it.

"Up and down Coyote will wander," they sang, "shake him by the leg," (they did) "shake him by the tail," (they did).

I howled and stumbled forward backward zigzagging now right now left clapping my paws together and baring my teeth then felt it, stars shooting by or maybe moons me riding on waves tripping over clouds rising up out of my belly trying to speak but words all liquid some crazy geyser that shot out through my throat them screaming that it was a goat a goat something stranded there before me I was past troubling and closed my eyes and fell asleep.

Rudy Trujillo

You won't find a nicer guy than me. You just won't. Now, I don't mean to say that I won't do my duty. Because I will. No one does their duty like me, even if it causes me pain to do it. I get no pleasure out of handcuffing people or sticking my gun in their ribs, and even less if I have to pull the trigger. But the state pays me a hundred and sixty-three bucks a week and I have to earn that money somehow. That's tax payer money and I've got to earn it, the whole damned burrito, or I'm just not doing my duty.

Now, being a public functionary in this county is no kid's play. Some of the residents just aren't that nice. Put out your hand for a shake and you'll get bitten. Which is not to say that everyone is rotten. There are probably some lovely people around here. Only thing is, if there are, I haven't met them, and I've met just about everyone and thrown about half of them in jail and given citations to the other half.

So, just doing my duty you understand, I stopped in on Gilbert, because one has to respect family ties no matter how strained they are and ours was about as strained as a size B bra on Dolly Parton's big sister. He sure hadn't acted much like a brother, but for all that I wasn't about to hit him over the head with a shovel and bury him in a shallow grave.

I slid up in front of his store, took a little smell of the bottle of Schenley I kept in the glove box, and climbed out. The sign on the door said closed, but his car was there, so that meant he was too. It was unlocked and I walked in.

"Gilbert."

"Rudy."

"You look like hell."

"I'm fine."

His puss was all beaten up and grinning in a pity-me sort of way and I asked him who did it to him.

"You've got to tell me, Gilbert, not only because I'm your brother, but because I'm also the law around here and these kinds of things have to be reported. Did they rob you?"

"There was only one."

"Okay, did he rob you?"

"She—He—well, yes, he took some things."

"What sort of things?"

"Four bottles of McKesson's elixir of terpin hydrate with codeine."

I took out a butt and lit it.

"Robbing a pharmacy during daylight hours is a serious crime, Gilbert. You're embarrassed and didn't want to tell anyone. I don't blame you. But we need to catch that son of a bitch."

Gilbert stiffened up when he heard me talk that way. He was a gentle bastard.

"No. Just leave it. It's nothing."

"Like hell it's nothing." I knocked some ashes onto the

floor. "You've been assaulted and robbed. In my county. This isn't about you anymore, this is about me. I can't have this party going around beating people up and stealing their elixir of terpin hydrate, least of all when it belongs to my brother. Now, you don't need to tell me the why or the details that led up to the situation. I neither need nor want to know them, but you better tell me who the party is."

"I don't want your help," he said shaking his head.

"I know what you want and I know what you got. I realize you're soft on the outside and soft on the inside but you better realize that this lump of tin on my shirt means I can do whatever the hell I want to. Now, Gilbert, you give me a name or I'm going to quit being nice to you."

"Cleopatra."

"What?"

"He calls himself Cleopatra."

"Jesus Christ Gilbert. If you weren't my brother I'd lock you up."

"After he got the first bottle from me the other day, I saw him get in a truck with Elmer. They were coming out of the Jiffy Shop and then drove away."

"Elmer?"

"Elmer Roybal."

I knew who he was talking about. That skinny long-haired bastard who had never worked a day in his life and who was out there doing his best to breed with his own aunt—a girl named Ramona who I had given a parking ticket to a few years earlier but hadn't seen around in a while. I couldn't really remember if her cake was good or not. I didn't know where Elmer lived—didn't know if he had a place to live—but I knew where her house was, out in that five-shack village, and I had to do something to keep busy.

"Okay. I'll take care of it. Just keep your mouth shut and I'll take care of it."

"My mouth is shut."

"It doesn't look that way to me."

"It is."

"You got any black beauties?"

"I can't keep giving them to you, Rudy."

"Sure, you'd give some fey named Cleopatra the whole damned drug store, but your own brother asks you for something to help him with his weight problem . . ."

He went and got the pills and gave them to me.

I sighed as I went out to my car. There's nothing easy about doing one's duty. There's nothing easy about being a public servant and having to drive thirty miles along a mule trail just to look into the matter of an assault and battery. Because that was the charge. Assault and battery and illegal usage of a government controlled substance and I guess there'd be resisting arrest, assaulting a police officer and anything else I could think of between here and there—in the name of duty, you understand.

It was already past noon. I had only had coffee and a sweet roll for breakfast. So I first stopped at Tiny's. There were a couple of old timers at the counter and some guy in one of the booths with his back to me. I sat in one of the free booths and ordered a rare hamburger and a bottle of beer.

"Drinking on duty?" Carla, the waitress, said. She wasn't

young. She was forty if she was a year and looked like she had been around the track more times than a greyhound bitch.

"Look, sister. Worry about getting enough tips to feed those four or five kids you got in that shed of yours before the state takes them away and let me worry about my own sobriety."

"Oh, you were planning on tipping today? I guess that means you'll be paying your tab too while you're at it."

"Why you——"

What was the use? I waved her away and she turned and wagged her fat tail at me so I could see what she had. Five minutes later a plate with a burger and some fries on it was shoved in front of me and a bottle of beer slammed down next to it. I took the top half of the bun off and looked down at about the thinnest looking hamburger patty I had seen in my life hiding under a slice of tomato and some onions. Every time I went in there that patty kept getting smaller and smaller. I reckoned pretty soon they'd just be serving me bread and onions.

I ate it. It wasn't good, and it sure as hell wasn't rare, but I ate it.

I used the can and then made tracks back to my car and, after having a short one just to wash the taste of the burger out of my mouth, slipped my sunglasses on and headed out. I kept my foot light on the pedal. There was no need to hurry. Either he would be there or he wouldn't, and I didn't really care either way. I was just biding my time till dinner. That burger had left me hungrier than before. I wondered where I'd go. I thought about Gilda's, but figured she probably wouldn't spot me a meal and I only had two dollars in my wallet and had been bouncing checks all week.

It's no wonder some cops turn crooked, I thought. Of course even if I wanted to it would have been hard to have got much graft on my beat. If there's no money, there's no money.

I stuck my hand in my pocket, took out the bottle of pills. They were supposed to control my appetite, so what the hell. The label said something about not using with alcohol, while driving, operating heavy machinery, not to take more than two in twenty-four hours, the usual bird song. I shuffled three into the palm of my hand, jacked them into my mouth and washed them down with a sip of Schenley.

I rolled into town, crossing myself as I passed Our Lady, then took another smell of the bottle to clear my head for business.

Elmer's truck was parked in front. I nosed my car up next to his, cut off the engine, opened the door and slid out. The screen door was closed but the door behind it open. I knocked on the screen door, waited about five seconds and knocked a second time only harder. I heard something stirring inside, then Elmer wandered up to the door, opened it and came out. He wasn't wearing a shirt and looked greasy as hell, like he hadn't shaved in about a year and hadn't washed up in longer. His eyes had a scared, furtive look to them. He was guilty, I didn't know of what, but he was guilty. I could see another figure moving around back there in the dark interior of the house. It looked like a woman—probably his aunt. I told Elmer that I needed to talk to him.

"Okay boss, but why?"

"I'll ask the questions here, thanks. If you would just step away from the house."

We stepped away from the porch. He seemed uncomfortable. I looked at him for about three seconds before talking.

"Where is he?" I asked.

He opened his eyes wide like he didn't know what I was referring to.

"Where is who?" he said.

I smiled and pushed the sunglasses back on my nose. I sort of hoped he would make it difficult for me. I had plenty of time before supper, and would just as soon have spent it working the hell out of Elmer as anything else.

"Look, Elmer. I knew you were stupid, but I didn't know you were so stupid as to be harboring a fugitive. I guess that means that you want to be accessory to his crime. I guess that means that you were as guilty of assaulting my brother and ripping him off earlier as he was."

"Earlier? What happened earlier?"

Now he really did look surprised. Either his acting skills had gone up about four hundred percent in the last four minutes or something really had caught him off guard.

"Sure. Earlier. And before that he was last seen with you. Getting into your truck. Positively identified."

He stood silent staring at the ground. I thought it was about time to give him a little personal counseling. He was taller than me, but skinny. He had probably knifed a few people, and maybe knocked out the teeth of a woman before, but I doubt he had ever really hit a man.

I set my hand gently on his shoulder and pulled him a little toward me. My knee lurched up between his legs. Then, while he was grabbing his nuts in what appeared to be genuine agony, I gave him a beautiful left directly under his jaw. His head flew back and he sort of sprang off his feet before hitting the ground.

"Gee, I'm sorry," I said. "My hand must have slipped."

"You bas——"

"What was that? Did you say something?"

I contemplated him as he struggled up and stood a little unsteady on his feet.

"Listen," he began and then his right eye sort reached out for my fist and the two kissed so I could almost hear the sucking sound and there he was back on the dirt. For about nine seconds I thought I had kayoed him, but then one of his hands started twitching a little, one of his eyes opened while the other was there squinting, and he tried to sit up. I put the heel of my boot against his chest and pushed him back down, then put the toe of my boot on his Adam's apple and applied pressure. "Boss," he gurgled. One hand was grabbing at my leg and the other was flopping around on the dirt. I pressed down a little bit harder and then eased up.

"Now, about Cleopatra," I began.

His tongue lapped at his lips. Then he started talking. At first I couldn't tell what he was really saying. Something about witches and Spaniards and picking up a stranger and crucifixion and the Montoya boy told him that. Then, little by little, I started getting the gist of the thing. I am not saying I believed it, but I understood the incoherent bean-head and thought maybe I had hit him a little too hard.

I looked over and saw an old woman staring at us from her front porch down and across the way. I didn't really care what she saw, but I also wasn't giving a rendition of Hamlet. I wasn't going to be the local entertainment. I offered Elmer my hand and pulled him to his feet.

"So there's gold, huh?" I asked.

"Don't say it too loud, the old lady might hear us."

Then Ramona came out. I looked her up and down. She was wearing jeans and a blouse that let me know pretty clearly she was a bit understaffed in the titty division, but I decided I wouldn't hold it against her. Her stems looked like they were okay, so that let her off the hook to some degree for the flat breastworks. I remembered her as being someone more attractive, but hadn't seen her in a while, and in this country a woman can slide rather fast.

"Your boyfriend slipped and hurt himself," I told her.

"He's my nephew."

"You don't say? I just thought——well, I was asking him about that fellow who was with him. Cleopatra, I think his name is."

She was quiet and had a hungry look in her eye. She had that scared, hungry look. I had seen it in quite a few women and it always excited me.

I licked my lips and told Elmer to get lost.

He said something and I made a quick motion and he was climbing into his heap. Ramona went into the house and came out with a shirt and handed it to him through the window. He probably wanted to kill me, and I couldn't blame him. But he was a coward. I motioned him away and he started the engine and gave me a lost look and then turned his head and the truck struggled along down the road.

I thought it was time I properly introduced myself to the lady.

"My name's Rudy Trujillo," I said.

"I know who you are."

My eyes stripped her naked. No, she didn't have hooker hips or anything like that, but she was probably still good for a tumble. It was my duty to put the play on her and I was just trying to figure out the angle when she told me I should leave.

"I don't think I could do that, ma'am," I said. "I'm not sure you would be safe here by yourself. One: your nephew is a violent man and might come back and hurt you. Two: you have a wanted fugitive running around somewhere. A nutjob who thinks he's Cleopatra. You and Elmer sent him off to be crucified, which apparently he was, and I would guess he probably doesn't think too well of you."

"It was Elmer's idea."

"But you didn't stop him."

"I told him it was a bad idea. I told him there wasn't any treasure. I don't know Cleopatra and don't care what happens to him."

She set her lips tight.

"Sure." I grinned. "Anyhow, you don't need to worry. I'm not going to abandon you. I've got a bottle in my car that we can have for dinner and maybe after you can provide a little dessert."

I went and got the bottle and went inside and she followed me.

"Have a seat," I said.

"Thanks, but I'll stand."

"Suit yourself, but the show might be pretty long," I said and settled down in a chair and gave her a strong look.

Now, this young lady was neither young nor, as I've already said, especially good-looking, but I had long ago quit being demanding about such things. It was not like I was going to enter her in a beauty contest or something. Sometimes a man simply needs female companionship and is willing to be forgiving and I figured she would probably appreciate a little attention.

I took a drink straight from the bottle and got a butt going.

"You been sleeping with your nephew again?" I asked.

It's funny how most women won't answer when you ask them a serious question. They go on and on about how they want their men to be truthful and straightforward, but ask them a direct question . . .

"There's nothing wrong with that," I continued. "Nothing wrong with it in principle, though it's a sloppy way to live. It all depends on who your nephew is I suppose. But if I were you——"

"I never slept with him."

"Sure you didn't. You're just lonely and need some company. A couple of witches across the street. A couple of old farmers. Hell, if I were you, I'd probably think Elmer was good company too."

She didn't say anything and I asked her if she wanted a drink. She said that she didn't.

"We don't have to drink from the bottle. Go and get some glasses. Sit down. Make yourself comfortable. Let's be friends. I'm not stuck up. I don't have anywhere to go. I'll just sit here and if the Queen of the Nile comes along, I'll protect you. Did anyone ever tell you that you're pretty? Well, you are. You're eyes are really something you know."

It was like stirring a pot of cold beans and trying to make it hot. Well—they weren't going to get hot, but better to eat cold beans than go hungry.

She went to the kitchen, got a glass and banged it down in front of me.

Theodore's Shovel

I like the dust but dust is always with me invasion of the bean crop farm birds dying mountain to mountain death is more beautiful birds dust agricultural dust putting my nose into it and then sell me took me a bit of yellow taken out of his hands for other things started digging and digging for dirt and dust rubbing in my nose out of it or not but I'm dead mountain agriculture in the mountains of dead birds is always a beautiful new soil and dust like digging me out of his hand to take any other thing is start digging can feel his hands I like dirt but dirt doesn't always like me never intentionally leaned buried manure anyone farm crops of beans can more beautiful agricultural you are hard and birds die in the mountains birds die in the mountains and dirt digging dirt you are hard and dry then took me and dug for other things some yellow took me in his hands and started digging dust and dirt but I like it or not I always beautiful birds in the mountains of agriculture thick manure dead bird dead in the mountains to dig soil and dirt and then took me and some other things to dig gold took me in his hands stick my head deep in there and started digging and then I do not like dust dust from the dust of the mountain is beautiful birds die of goat farm corn in the mountains of death and the invasion of my bean crops agricultural dust constantly heading away and then took me to my next things started by digging for dirt and dust and a bit of money taken from his corn hands for digging is not for sale mountain agriculture is always my pile of dead birds dead new soil and beautiful like the dust from his hands to dig because manure I can take another start digging but I like the earth earth is anyone I never intentionally dig the soil in the mountains like a bird more beautiful than the birds of agricultural vehicles are constantly entering and I took the hurt but I dig the money in his hand no money and I started to dig the dust and dirt it corn also likes to dig dirt the corn and dead birds of the mountain is always beautiful birds of agriculture in the mountains if we could plant you golden kernels I am not dead then take some other thing to me is finding gold in his manure hand my nose is going down some rays of sun in his hand taking began digging then we can die by the bean crop farm in the mountains to die for the other things I found and he took.

Our Little Lady of the Trunk

Women feel stronger emotions than men and yes I hate the miserable little sinner though I know I am not supposed to hate or have vexation of spirit yet I strongly dislike the way he walks by and wags his head at me a woman filled with spirit (it is after all something that should be respected).

Travelling travelling never moving yet travelling. Time sweeping me with its wings sun rising and setting. Yes, women feel strong emotions though the expression on my face never changes unless by shadow by time seen winter days and spring days and summer days (I do like to see the blue skies and birds flying you cannot blame me for that).

I am made of plaster. Some object painted, painted by hand (though beautifully I do believe) who has stood silently for many years in the shade of my little alcove. The old women leave me flowers (nothing fancy) and the young men leave me cigarettes. I take what I can get, which is only natural for a woman who is standing alone. And I perform miracles when I can. When the mood hits me or I want to or I am fond of someone—though I am never too fond of anyone, since that is an earthly emotion. After Maria Martinez brought me three hard-boiled eggs, I got rid of her son's lisp. It is not my fault that he later got stabbed in the neck. At least he died with right speech some crows flying above and the wind gently sweeping his soul away (the wrong way). Then later Francisco Jaramillo came and asked me to punish his brother for sleeping with his wife. He left me a pack of Winston cigarettes and a bottle of beer and the next day Juan was kicked in the stomach by a mule and he died three days later. So I do what I can when I can (holding faith, and a good conscience).

There used to be more children around. When they would come along by themselves, I would tell them about the beast with ten horns with its stench of evil and sound of fornication and they would cry. I have always liked to see children cry. The world, after all, must cry for *My* Son.

When Theodore Montoya wanted a child though, he never came to me. I know he was out there offering liquor to L 5 Flower yet none to me. A little shameful of him. I'm as thirsty as the rest though I would never do anything in excess. And yes, he got a child, yet what a child some real rotten fruit of the womb.

The boy would walk by me day after day. I tried to tell him about the beast eating the whore's flesh, but he just laughed. I never liked how he looked at me (could see that his prankishness was obscene and even dangerous). If he had spoken to me nicely, even offered me an apple, a cob of corn, or a few flowers (women do need to be shown appreciation sometimes), I would have treated him well. I would have blessed him, despite my feelings. If he had been a little girl, I have no doubt he would have done so, and incidents that were to cause me so much pain would have never occurred. Remember mothers, having a boy is not always a good thing!

It was another day of me standing waiting and watching. By ten in the morning it was quite warm by noon rather hot by two uncomfortable yet I was still cool, ready to hear of other's sorrows and pain, to offer my boons and blessings. Is all I ever wanted was a little acknowledgement. For people to just acknowledge how much I have done and how much I could do if they would only let me because I did (after all) receive the charge.

So again he came walking along, triumphantly, some miniature Tamburlaine, wagging his stick, skipping with his feet (I have noticed that only brats skip).

If he had only continued on. But no, on this occasion, bolstered by his inflated ego (I believe), he stopped in front of me and, with arms akimbo (to use an expression I am none too fond of but which is nonetheless evocative), spoke.

"You are always standing here staring at me when I walk by," he said. "I don't like it. You are always trying to scare me."

I smiled yet did not reply, hardly thought he was worth replying to. His insolence was rather remarkable. This was, after all, my place and not his. It was I who had performed miracles and not he. I who was the darling of the little town yes and sometimes little birds came and rested at my feet because they trusted me. Why would I try to scare the little man?

"Stop smiling."

I smiled. It was the slightest of smiles, but a smile nonetheless.

"If you don't stop it, I'm going to hit you," he said. "Hit

you with my stick."

The vulgarity of the child amazed me. He could threaten me, a woman, if he liked, yet I would not reply to either dreadful insults or blasphemies. I was determined to ignore him, and looked on, as if he were not there, as if I were looking at some far away land where people were couth. I supposed (always thinking better of people than they really are) that he would never really carry out his threat. How wrong I was, how very wrong I was.

Lifting up his stick he did exactly what he had threatened to do, bringing it down with great force on my left arm, which cracked and fell away. At first, I could hardly believe what had happened, that wickedness could exist in such quantity. That a gracious woman could be waylaid in broad daylight and beaten in such a manner. A stinging sensation went through me.

"You shouldn't hit a woman!" I shrieked, but he just laughed, laughed and kept laughing.

I looked down at my arm which was now lying on the ground and felt shame and (I must say) hostility.

And he answered me, saying, "You have been cheating people long enough. You think you are powerful, but look what my stick can do to you."

The boy's brutality was horrible. He lifted up the stick again. I thought he would not dare hit me a second time, would not dare to continue assaulting a woman who had not done him the least harm (my faith in the good, though always belied, is never ending). But I under-, or should I say *over*-estimated him.

I saw the stick descending. It hit me on the side of the

head and the world spun around me. I felt dizzy. I looked to right and left. To the right I saw the sky above. To the left, the earth below. Half my mouth was pressed against the dirt. My head (poor thing) had gone tumbling to the ground, and it was as if I were stripped of my glory. For an instant I saw him. Picking up my fallen arm, his laughter loud, loud and then tapering off, receding into the distance. I believe he was skipping as he went away. I was speechless. Appalled. Surely I was blushing, my cheeks more ruddy than rubies (yes, I was embarrassed, I will admit that).

It was more than just pain, it was sorrow. Because there is beauty that doesn't stand still and goes away bit by bit and beauty which flies off all at once (or is knocked off in this case). Would people leave offerings or pray to a beaten up thing like me? Could I blame them if they did not? A woman with only one arm, whose head was in a rather precarious state? No wonder it is that sometimes statues cry, no miracle in that (if you knew our sorrow) and no miracle if I would temporarily remove myself and ask not for revenge but retribution (though the damage had been done).

No, I am not vengeful (never have been) yet do believe in justice. He should have never presumed to make me his enemy. An angel he was not.

Yes, blood would pursue him, as was only fitting. There was no use in appealing to my God (who had little power in those parts and in general was rather slow for my taste), yet appeal I would, even if the fellow didn't have a rainbow on his head. I was privy to the mysteries of all these sorts of things, and knew just where to find his creator (I was now feeling around with my one arm trying so hard to prevail).

I am sorry if I seem disloyal. I am not, yet when a woman is in distress she must resolve the situation however she can. Wisdom, they say, is a woman.

Elmer Roybal

It hurts. It hurts.

My eye.

So what, boss? Okay you can't take the love in my heart away from me I get in my truck and drive away being pushed around but only so far they can't take my love. They can't take it from me but I can't see very well out of one eye. I won't let them take her from me throwing myself over the dirt road and then about twenty minutes later sliding along the pavement I have $4.26 in my pocket and some food stamps but I don't want food less than a quarter tank of gas but I don't care if I run out I could kill myself but no one would care next thing I'm at the hardware store falling out of my truck time to nail my head together plastic cement I get two cans.

"What are you going to do with that?"

"Model airplanes."

"You'll have to show me your collection sometime. By the amount of this stuff you buy, you must have thousands."

"Yeah."

"One hit you in the eye?"

As soon as I'm back in the truck I'm opening it feeling the hot air go into me look at myself in the rear view mirror I don't look so bad but the eye sure is black well if he's alive where is he did he find it someone's casting spells I can feel it that much I'm sure now I'm driving again can't even feel the gas pedal but it must be there because I'm moving stop at the liquor store inside he looks at me my face and is talking to me.

"Looks like someone thought your face was a football, Elmer." I can see his teeth.

I don't answer. "A pack of Lucky's and a miniature of Seagram's Seven."

"One?"

"Three."

"That'll be one dollar and eighty-five cents."

"Do you take food stamps?"

"Does this look like food?"

"I'll give you five dollars worth of stamps, boss."

"Well . . ."

"And a pack of matches too, boss."

So I'm stepping outside lighting a smoke can hardly taste it but I'm smoking it and now back in the truck tug out one of the miniatures and drink it in two swallows I'm going to kill him I think I'm going to kill him. Okay. What's he doing with her anyhow we'll go away together drive to California I snap the cigarette butt out of the truck window and keep going I must have driven this road a million times but just one last time if I could get her and go. She's mine, I discovered her.

Now I'm out of the truck and wandering in the trees the cement in one hand I keep breathing it and thinking looking around and thinking thoughts just moving around in a circle I can't see out of one eye.

Then the sky starts changing color, becoming soft and pink and I can see them, the angels flying around in the sky and I wave and they wave back, now I am on a mission. You can't let them do it to you take it away. Everything's in my head and I sit down can feel the earth moving under me it's melting but still cold generation after generation healing pigs and chickens I could sleep in the truck but I wasn't tired thinking about what could be if I could just man up to it their grandfather had buried it boarded up the church and every time I saw Ramona it was like having my heart in my mouth. I take another whiff am rubbing my cheek in the dirt and take another whiff you don't need to snicker at yourself like that my one eye wrapped around a stone.

I fall back in the cab of the truck turn on the ignition going slow because I have to be patient almost on empty now. I stop to see Our Lady but her head is knocked off arm is knocked off so I have a Seagram's it fits right into my world.

I'm crying. Tears are coming out of both eyes and I'm crying. I put the can of cement at her feet and also a cigarette can feel the blood running from my eyes and I look down at her broken off head and blood is coming from her cheek and still coming from my eyes her neck is bloody I wish I could dance with her.

I can remember.

"Dios te salve llena eres de gracia el Señor es contigo bendita tú eres entre todas las mujeres y bendito es el fruto de tu vientre Jesús Santa María ruega por nosotros, pecadores ahora y en la hora de nuestra muerte."

And me and her start talking she tells me the Blue Boy is no good they're going to get rid of Blue Boy Montoya. That's fine. Why not everything is soft I can feel my hands are dough then it was dark my tears fall on the ground and are sparkling there and I put the can up to my face and breathe some more the stars are like spot-lights shining on me my face is glowing and set it back down in front of her leave it for her me there in front of her kissing her feet I'm going to do it going to do it breathe some more then get out of my truck my legs are long rubbery they stretch out a great distance maybe even miles with my arms I can reach up and touch the sky if I could pull down the moon I would eat it.

Now I'm sitting, I'm sitting.

I swallow another miniature it's tasteless.

"You've got to get her. Dig up the money and get her. Take the truck all the way to California. Siphon some gas from somewhere. Drive up right on the beach and get out and sleep on the sand."

The voice is my own and it's talking to me. I'm taking another whiff and it's talking to me. Everything's frozen. Hot and frozen. Now the hills are getting light I've been sitting here all night.

What was that?

It's telling me to use the crowbar pry her away.

Conway

I woke up in the afternoon. Another hot day. All sun, no shade.

Shade.

Perhaps you need to think about hope.

Reverse the things.

They hung her from the tree. One color.

They took her hung her upside down the blood dripping down and skinned her. She was the only one I ever loved.

Tulip.

How can you live so long after that so long after.

Routine. Hanging up wet.

Then they took me far away and let me loose. I stood under the sky and cried out. Should have left. But found my way home.

I don't remember when I was born or if I was born.

Rubbing my horns against a post.

Never maybe. I've watched them become old.

Sometimes on a full moon they rode me. But even that was routine. They wouldn't let me see her. Something about me making her milk smell. But then they killed her. The old man killed her.

Tulip.

She expands.

They ate her. Then I could feel. Smudgy faction of blood. And then later when the old man died Candelaria came out and rode me. From time to time on my throne.

Her legs.

They might taste like dandelions.

I should have kicked her then thrown her then but maybe I still had hope. And then it was us under the moon she was holding my horns us under the moon were we children then. And then we had it.

I woke up in the afternoon.

No dandelions.

The boy was there. With a man. Pointing at me. The man climbed over the fence. Cautiously. Pulling. He was untying me and leading me away. Fine.

The boy. He had brought me sweet corn.

Sweet corn.

There was the boy. With one person. The pounding sun behind you.

No sweet corn.

I sat down and watched. Let him dig.

Quiet boy.

The dirt flew up in the air. I closed my eyes. Excavation. Leave him to dig. Then she was there with me. Still young. She was still young and there with me. Tulip us chewing fresh grass together the grass was high in the meadow she was chewing it and walking in front of me turning her head and chewing. That stillness.

Tulip was chewing some sunshine on her back I could smell her it was good.

Let him dig you.

The coyote and the boy were talking. Type of revolutions.

Then it was there too. Another boy. The same boy. He was still young and there too. Speech and the boys.

Been here so long. Ride me I'll go slow.

Closed my eyes. Didn't care to listen. Then I felt something. Picking me up scraping against me some comb could feel falling but too lazy. Almost hurts opened them but all was dark. Soft and dark. Warm and dark. Moist and dark.

Looked for dandelions.

I moved my hind legs but soon couldn't move them anymore my head in some kind of puddle.

In order to examine if the barrel but couldn't really move.

It was dark and I closed my eyes and fell asleep.

Rocking me slowly. If I could smell her. Chewing tall grass walking with me and chewing. Moving.

Hot and dark. Humid and dark.

Grumbling. Moved my nose.

Then I could smell it. Beautiful.

I was wet all over please be made.

I tried to stretch but couldn't but I could lick. And I licked around me. Smelled it and licked around me. More sweet than the sweetest corn where was she? Shift my legs behind my head in a type of magma. Still young and there with me. She was chewing it and walking in front of me turning her head. Moving around and around.

That is slain.

Tulip.

Pushing around me. Soft hot and wet. Pushing against

my head and horns. Pushing me up could feel them sharp again and warm.

I fell out, wet all over.

The rear side of the sun. Cycles.

Everything was soft. Clay. Clouds. I have moved could feel this. Good. The trees made sound.

Clouds.

I wandered around. Looking for Tulip.

Where was she? I don't remember. Wet and cloud. It is this before me. I am aware of this movement. Perhaps you need to think about hope and reverse the things.

The grass along the high pasture.

Tulip.

Patricio Chávez

I stood in the darkness and watched. When the lights went off I still watched. So filled with love you couldn't call it hate. No. Have to keep it for myself.

The day had been like it was carved out of stone. I had waited for the night and stood in it like I was standing in outer space. Sometimes I can't feel anything around me. It is like I am dropping. One day I'll be on the madero because it has to be like that. My head will be everything.

A man walked down the street. Who was it? To Ramona's house, cop car sitting in front. She would never let me in. It's become a village of whores. When we get the land grant back we'll clean it all up.

Time to clean things up.

They were an original family but a curse. And no more women came. Now the good times were gone.

So I stood in the darkness and watched. I'd do it with the cop right there practically across the road. It's my land. I was standing on it in outer space.

My heart felt like a rocket. I could ride it all the way through.

They wouldn't do it wouldn't let me be up there. To receive the grace. Some ungrateful man ungrateful witch. Since I was seventeen. I had brought ten candles. Let the blood run since I was seventeen up at the morada I bowed my head thinking if I could one day go up to Calvary a big nail through my arm.

It would drip down. If I could drink from a sponge.

They took me in there blindfolded and after giving me the cuts gave me three lashes. I asked for more, but they only gave me three. When the blindfold was off I saw my thighs were wet with blood.

This is the gift that the Lord gives you as you were deceived.

I was so happy. I was wounded.

The good times.

It is only good times. My knife will alert you. It will alert you to death. It will alert you to death but again I become a sinner. A sinner filled with love to transform your hate. You have to drink the wine to feel drunk.

I took off my boots and socks, set them down by where the Devil lived and walked barefoot. The soles of my feet felt the dirt and sharp little rocks.

I went to the back door, opened it and went in. Moonlight spilled in the window. Everything was still. I remembered Serafin Lucero. I had sat on a boulder and shot him as he drove by. Never told anyone. Went home and ate stew. You keep this happiness to yourself.

Moonlight was spilling in the window. The light was so clear I felt like drinking it.

The dining table. It would become part of the land grant too. I'd take it on my back.

And they'd fall by the sword. The next room was very dark but my eyes adjusted. The photo of Vicente Griego.

I couldn't see his face but knew he was looking. My heart apologized. I manned myself up and went into the first bedroom.

It was like reaching in a well. I took the knife out and stepped forward, feeling with my left hand. The edge of the bed. Then the blanket under my fingers.

I stopped. I was breathing.

I heard a voice that said to go ahead. It hadn't been her who shunned me. It had been her sister. But still. Serafin had done me wrong and I had eaten him like a lion. But with her it was different but if I did one I had to do them both.

I was biting on my bottom lip.

The voice said to go ahead. So I did. I was full of love and I did it, like a string was attached to my hand and someone else was pulling it. Trembling. My hand was trembling like a dove. I listened, thought I could hear the falling of the blood. I could hear my own lungs and then left and went through the living room to the other room.

The bed looked small, almost like a child's. But she was little bigger than a child.

It didn't matter. She was an old woman when I was born so I entrusted myself to God. He gave it to my hand.

Looking down, I saw the white face in a pool of white hair.

It was like stabbing at some bag of bones. There was nothing there. Just dust that was rising up and the smell of dust. The sweat was jumping out of my pores. But I had done it. I looked at the shape of the cross above the bed and fell to my knees.

I cried. I sat on the floor and cried.

Cleopatra

One thing about terps. It gives the world a brighter color. It makes the impossible seem real and makes one feel a little closer to Tawaret and Tefnut.

I had drunk down the first bottle as soon as I got out of the shop, right there in the street, and it had eased the pain in my hands and steadied my mind. Then I went to the grocery next door and got myself a bottle of Frost 8/80 Dry White Whisky, a bottle of Heaven Hill Old Style Bourbon and a fresh pack of smokes. I thought about getting food, but decided against it. I hadn't eaten in a while, but didn't feel like getting take away from the store and chowing down on some curb. I needed to in a chair. Eat like a human being. My hands hurt and the haunted feeling was still with me some dream not sure if I was awake or asleep, the lights, the cross, me nailed to it.

I walked a little and opened the bottle of bourbon and took a slug. It went down my throat like a horse through a mouse hole. My nerves were all shot to hell. I lit a cigarette.

Okay. It was the middle of the day and I was in some little hick town and all of this was no stranger than other things that had happened to me. Maybe less strange. I looked up. The sky was staring at me in the face, its blue eyes just staring at me calmly as ever. It made me feel like running, but I didn't.

I took another slug. This time it tasted pretty good. Why the hell should I run when I could walk?

I was starting to feel a little better and moved slowly down the road.

About two blocks down there was a lunch joint and I went in and sat in a booth. I felt like a pastrami sandwich but they didn't have that, so I ordered a ham sandwich and a Coke.

"What happened to your hands?" the waitress asked staring at them.

"My car overheated about a mile from here and when I was taking the cap off the radiator I burned them."

"Not much of a mechanic, are you?"

"Nope."

She went off to get my chow and I got up with my bag and went to the restroom. It was narrow and half-way clean and under the sink was stashed a tool chest with some extra rolls of toilet paper on top of it.

I undid the shirt swaddling around my hands. The wounds looked a little purple and ugly. I washed my hands with water then poured some hydrogen peroxide over them. It stung and foamed. I wrapped an Ace bandage around each hand. I must have looked like some pug on his way to the Colosseum.

An idea was in the back of my mind. I looked in the tool chest which had a few things and got out a screwdriver and a pair of pliers and put them in my pocket. I took a slug of bourbon remembering that boy whose arms had been blown off some breeze of the Nile Delta.

I went back to my booth. A Coke was already sitting there for me and about three minutes later I got my sandwich. I had worked my way through half of it when a cop came in. I glanced over my shoulder just long enough to take in the straight-ticket Republican piglet face and turned away.

The waitress came and I was afraid she was going to suggest that I ask the cop for help or offer to call a tow truck or something but she didn't. She just asked if I wanted dessert and I told her no thanks, just a cup of coffee. I drank it slowly and she refilled it and I started in on that. When I heard the door swing and felt the pig go I asked for the check and after paying threw fifty cents on the table for tip.

I wandered outside. Turned left off the main drag. Some ugly houses were placed along it like a bum with half his teeth knocked out.

A bird was singing somewhere. There were a few trees and I looked up at them but didn't see anything. I suppose for the bird it was a good day, but hearing it singing made me feel sort of sad, alone. Why was it singing on such a damned ugly street?

Maybe it was the bird's mating call I was hearing. I wondered if it would have any luck.

The mating call of humans isn't quite so eloquent and what was my mating call, just standing there with a sack of bottles in my hand, how could anyone ever care about me but maybe someone could.

Maybe.

I got to thinking. I got to thinking about that gold.

Maybe the kid wasn't making it up. Maybe Elmer had been right. Why not? The Spanish had come here in the early days and maybe there really was some treasure left over that those damned witches were looking after and the other three, maybe they hadn't known. Anyhow things were already so crazy anything seemed possible.

And there was her. She was the maybe with a capital M. Could I really just move on without seeing her again? I probably could. But I didn't want to. Sure, I would be a fool to go back, but I had been a fool most of my life and didn't see any reason to stop now. You have to dream a little if you want to live.

Not just remember, but also dream.

If there really was some gold, I'd need a way to get it out of there. I could always take Elmer's truck, but there was the risk that Elmer would come with it. Even if I said no, Ramona might insist on it. And there was only room for two people in my dream, and Elmer was not one of them. Not by a long shot, so I needed a vehicle and I needed her and the treasure if there was any and that would be good, up at my palace in Cyprus, if father had once laughed the earth would have started to shake.

Well, I had been forming the idea since back in the diner.

It was a lousy street with lousy houses, but a couple of the cars weren't too bad. The one I wanted was down toward the end.

It was a late model Chevrolet, four door hardtop.

Now, taking someone's car in broad daylight is not exactly the safest thing one can do, but if they wanted me to do things the safe way they should have started me off differently. If I had lived safe I'd have probably been some kind of high priest grown fat, some clean shaven man at a desk quietly watching time go by.

The car was unlocked. I flopped the bag of bottles on the seat then snapped open the hood and had the thing started in about three minutes.

I pressed on the gas and swung it into the road, looking in the rear view mirror as I did so to see if anyone was coming after me. No one was. No one had noticed.

I took a right on the next corner and kept going, doing just about five miles over the legal speed limit.

Stealing a car was probably not the brightest thing I could have done. But things seemed to have always gone from bad to worse with me, and I guess I didn't feel like bucking the trend. Getting out of trouble in one place and into worse trouble in another. Some momentum that kept me steadily going in that direction, almost logically, like I was iron being dragged toward some far off magnet or hell I could almost still hear the ringing in my ears and then breathed deeply, calming myself.

It felt good to be behind the wheel. I looked at the gas gauge. It showed half a tank. The engine ran smoothly, like velvet. I rolled down the window and let the air swoop in over me. When I hit the dirt road I goosed her to about sixty and the car sailed over the ruts. If you went too slow the thing would rattle to pieces, but if you went fast enough and steered her right to avoid the really big potholes, you just sailed on.

I was thinking about Ramona. She surely knew she

had been putting me in danger. Or maybe she hadn't. I'm not sure it mattered either way. It didn't really change the way I felt about her. As crazy as it seemed I wanted to pull the pieces together and the best way to start was to forgive because I had seen something in her eyes and felt something was there.

I yanked the steering wheel to the left and bumped about a hundred yards down an offroad. I put the car in park, but kept it running.

After taking a slug of bourbon, I opened the glove box and looked at the registration. It belonged to one Raymond Martinez of 425 Luisa Street. Poor bastard.

I lit a smoke and opened a bottle of terps. After drinking half of it, I screwed the cap back on and slid it into my pocket.

My hands felt fine now. They were a bit clumsy, but they felt fine.

I threw the car in reverse and got back on the road. The sun was high up in the sky and as I went I kept trying to work it out. Forget about the past the sounds and pain just forget about that. There was her and the gold and if I could get them both that would be a beginning. Get the money and get her. And get out.

I sped past the walls of rock and sand that looked like obelisks or statues of Tut-Ench-Amun or Memnon, some seated giant. A Valley of the Kings, valley of the rubes and hicks.

A pick-up truck was coming toward me going the opposite direction, taking up half of both lanes. It swerved to the side as we neared and we passed each other. It was

Elmer but he was looking straight ahead, miserable and sullen, and didn't notice me.

I thought about turning around and tracking him down, but that's not what I was there for. I wasn't angry at him any more than at Ramona or those poor slobs who had been shooting at me and I'd been shooting back at their corpses there in the hot sun.

When I got near the village I slowed down. There was no need to draw attention to myself. I passed by the store and saw a little old man sitting in front. He waved and I waved back. A police cruiser was parked out in front of Ramona's place and so I just kept on going. That weasel back at the pharmacy had probably reported me and somehow they had traced me back here. Or maybe not. Maybe they were after Elmer. He was as liable to be in trouble as anyone else, more so, and maybe the cop was there looking for him and that's why Elmer had been speeding away looking miserable.

Maybe.

I didn't intend to find out. I kept on driving.

I went past the house of the old lady and the little windowless doorless structure and swung onto a small side road and kept going. I needed to find the kid. He knew where it was buried. The road went up past a few run-down looking farms, weeds growing high along the road, then dead-ended at a better looking place with smoke coming out of the chimney. I managed to turn around and started letting the car roll back down the road.

I saw the kid walking across a field toward me and took my foot off the gas. I threw the car in park, got out and walked up to him.

He was carrying the plaster arm of something in his hand.

"Want to make five dollars?" I said.

He asked what he had to do to make five dollars and I told him.

"I'll get my dad's shovel and show you where it is."

He threw the arm down and ran off. About ten minutes later he came back carrying a shovel, which he handed to me, and then picked back up the arm. I had the bottle of bourbon in one hand and the half-bottle of terps in my pocket and we walked down the road some and across a meadow to a goat pen. Inside was the oldest, ugliest looking goat I had ever seen. Two long horns curled out of its head. It looked over at us with blood-shot eyes. There was a little dilapidated shelter of sticks and old boards, but it was in front of the shelter rather than under it and the shelter didn't look like it would offer much protection from the elements anyhow.

"It's in there."

"In the goat pen?"

"Yes. Under where the goat is tied."

"Are you sure?"

"No."

I climbed over the fence into the pen and walked over to the goat. It was so old and beat up that it probably couldn't have rammed me if it tried.

My hands were already beginning to hurt again so I emptied the half-bottle of terps in my mouth and eased it down with a few slugs of the Heaven Hill. The sun was hovering above me like a torch. The goat was tied to a metal stake in the ground. I untied it and pulled at the rope, but the goat didn't want to move. I pulled harder and then it got up and I led it over to the side of the pen.

The place where the goat had been sitting was worn away to form a shallow, hard hollow.

I took off my shirt and started to dig. The kid sat on the fence and watched. The earth was hard, like it hadn't been turned for a long time, if ever. It was hard and dry. I wished I'd had a pick axe but didn't ask the kid for one. He had already gotten me the shovel and I didn't need to attract attention him running back every five minutes for tools.

I slammed the shovel in with my foot and chipped away at it. The dirt started piling up around me, me thinking maybe I was digging up Ramses II. Sweat was melting out of my pores. I was out of shape and could feel it in my lower back. I started to wonder if there was anything there. Probably not. I could drink all the bottles of terps in the state, but it wouldn't make a fairy tale real. Elmer was a liar and the kid was a kid, who could dream up all sorts of things he hadn't said he was sure it was even there and the last time I had dug anything had been back with the palm trees and could hear them whistle right by my head.

Lunching on dirt.

I had been in good shape then. Pulling stones up onto the pyramids to help the slaves. And even after and they were still killing themselves over there but at least I was out. I remembered lying in the bed but had told myself better to forget.

I looked up and the kid was gone now. The goat looked

like it was sleeping. Okay so keep digging unless you got something better to do. I didn't. I widened the hole a bit and went down further.

I don't know what time it was. Late in the afternoon I figured. I dug for a while longer, cursing audibly.

Then the shovel hit something hard. I thought it was a rock at first but eased up with the shovel and started digging around with my hands and saw the pot. It was painted with geometric designs in black. Like teeth. Okay, so I had been hurt, once before and once after and lots of little times in between. But now things were working out.

When I saw it, I didn't really know what it was, thinking okay I see now but if he had kept wandering around out in front it must have been for a reason maybe because he actually cared in his own way actually cared or maybe he just wanted to shoot me but no he didn't.

The sun was strong but was getting low and the sweat seemed like it was dripping over my eyes.

I cleared the dirt around it with my hands. It was fragile as hell. I worked at it for about two hours until it was finally free. Lifting it out by myself was no easy task, but I did it. I certainly wasn't going to ask anyone for help and there was no one to ask.

It must have weighed about two hundred pounds. The top was sealed with some kind of animal skin. I pierced it with the shovel and tore it away. Filled with golden nuggets and I touched them small and delicate.

It was twilight and I stood there and smiled and laughed.

I took my shirt and wrapped it around the top, tying it with the sleeves, then lifted it up out of the hole and rolled it on its side out of the goat pen and then over the field. It was pretty rough going, but finally I made it to the road. I looked back. The kid was over by the goat pen again. I waved, but he didn't see me. He was talking to some kind of jackal or maybe it was Anubis. I worked the jar up the road to the car and then opened the back door and muscled it into the back seat and undid the shirt and put it back on. But then it was spilling so I yanked the jar out and, with a fair amount of effort, worked it into the trunk.

I took out a bottle of terps, the third, and emptied it at a draught.

I still owed the kid five bucks, and went over to the goat pen and he was gone again and now so was the goat, but the bottle of Heaven Hill was there next to the hole, so I took a drink. It seemed like I could start to see my way out of some of these troubles. It had always been about feeding people and that was why the Nile had to be protected, because it was fertile. Maybe she was fertile too, but why was I thinking like that, you're hoping a little too much, I thought then I wet my mouth with the bottle again and closed my eyes could still see the bright flashes, flares going up everything suddenly illuminated oil popping out of pores my hands gummy with it.

I made my way back to the car. It was dark now and I sat on the hood. It was quiet and peaceful and then when you couldn't see them they could come at any time at any time it could come and hit you in the back or head or chest I saw him walking by slowly looking at the house I could see the pistol in his hand he had grown thin and his pants hung loose on him his head leaned forward I could feel it getting me the fear.

I'd leave the car there. I took a drink from the bottle of bourbon, a very long one, and then it was empty. But I wasn't drunk. I felt light and clear as I looked up at the nothingness of the night sky.

I took the bottle of Frost 8/80, opened it, and snapped a drink off the neck. Carrying it, I walked down the road over to where the houses were. None of them had light coming through the window but hers. The cruiser was still there in front. I walked up silently to the porch and looked through the window. A fat policeman was sitting in the living room with a drink in his hand. I recognized the straight-ticket Republican piglet face. Ramona was on the couch, her head cupped in her hands.

I breathed heavily, guessed that maybe there was no escaping any of it an image came of me being locked up in some country jail beating my head against the bars but I wouldn't let that happen and if he was there because of me, she shouldn't have to suffer for it, I had done enough of that to people.

I went around to the kitchen door, opened it and walked in and then through to the front room.

He looked around and I saw his eyes go from my face to my hands.

"Well, hello," he said and started getting up. He had a gun at his side and I thought he'd probably reach for it. I relaxed the bottle onto the floor and, stepping up, let go of my right, but he saw it coming so it only grazed the side of his face.

"Looks like we got a big boy here," he said touching his

face, and grinned. He could have gone for his gun then, but he didn't, was too confident in himself for that.

He was fat and out of shape, but he knew how to box and was remarkably fast, as some fat men are. I felt his right sink deep into my stomach like a block of cement and then his left sideswipe my chin and I think I heard him laugh. But even as my head was jolted to one side I was lunging at him, not worrying about his belly which had too much padding to make it worth jousting with, but going for whatever it was that was above his shoulders. I struck out with my left and chiseled his neck and then my right landed under his eye. His head sprang back and then forward like he was a puppet. He came at me with a strong right that I blocked and then I tried a judo chop on him, but he cut that off with his forearm. I began thrusting my fists at his face and neck and I could smell him, warm and putrid. But I had holes in my hands, and each blow probably hurt me more than him and my hands were bandaged and I was unable to use the necessary force. He waved his meat-hooks around in front of him then gave me a powerful one-two in the face. I felt his knee surge up between my legs and I sprang back in pain could see the lights going off in the jungle. He moved quickly, ruthlessly. His foot went up into my stomach and I was back against the wall, a thick chunk of dirty pain my mind out of focus, my shoulder pushing up against the picture of the Virgin Mary me up there wishing for resurrection.

"You fey son of a bitch," I heard him say.

I spit a little blood and he smiled. It looked like I might not be able to take him. I was fighting because I had to, but he was doing it because he enjoyed it, just like others I had met that were there because they liked killing, killing or hurting legally. He stood before me, legs apart. He had probably gone over a hundred guys like this, was probably just about the one thing he was good at.

"Back off." It was Ramona's voice.

She was standing there with a gun. His gun. I don't know how she had got it, but she had. She looked small, almost like a child.

He turned toward her.

"Now listen, Ramona," he started saying, kneading his fist into the palm of his hand.

"Get away from him or I'll pull the trigger," she said.

"Ramona."

"You wouldn't be the first cop to get shot around here."

"I don't think you could hit me if you pulled that trigger. You can only miss once. But I don't think you could hit me baby."

"We can find out," she said in a hard voice.

He backed away, a sullen look on his face.

I moved off from the wall and motioned for her to give me the gun, which she did.

"Now turn around," I said to him.

"Prefer to shoot me in the back?" he asked. His voice sounded almost like he was enjoying himself.

"I'm not going to shoot you if I don't have to. I don't need any more trouble."

"Well, at least we agree on that."

He turned around and I clobbered him with the butt of the gun on the back of the neck and he started turning toward me and I clobbered him again. Almost in slow motion he sunk to the floor, leaned forward and was there spread-eagle. I emptied his pockets. In his front he had a ring of keys and a few quarters. In his back he had a wallet with his badge and two one dollar bills. I took the keys and money and threw the empty wallet across the room.

I asked Ramona to help me and we dragged him over to the cast iron wood stove. I took his handcuffs off his belt and put one around his left wrist and the other around the hinge of the stove door. The only way he'd be able to move would be to pull the door off its hinges or pull the stove around with him. I put the keys in my pocket.

Ramona looked at my face and then at my bandaged hands.

"You're hurt," she said.

I went into the kitchen and felt the heat of the smaller stove in there and wondered if she always kept it going and then looked in the mirror. My mouth was bleeding. The basin was there and a bucket of water so I filled the basin from the bucket. I undid the bandages on my hands. The wounds still looked ugly so I washed my hands and washed my face with water. The basin filled with dirt and a little blood. There was even dirt in my ears and I cleaned them out. I looked in the mirror again. I looked tired, unshaven, ragged, but I had seen myself look worse.

Ramona came in.

"Want a drink?" she asked. She was staring at my hands.

"Sure. Make it tall."

I redid the bandages and she brought it to me and I drank half of it off at a swallow. It was Schenley.

"Do you have a sandwich or something?"

"I can fry you some eggs."

"Okay."

She started cooking. She asked me if I wanted coffee and I said no and finished off my drink.

The eggs smelled good.

"Fry me a couple too," a voice yelled from the next room. He was conscious.

She didn't. She fried three for me and put them on a plate with a piece of the flatbread.

I sat at the table in the front room and chowed down while the cop watched. She put the bottle of Frost 8/80 there in front of me, but I didn't feel like drinking any, so she brought me a glass of water and I drank that wading through some stagnant pool the huge leeches on my legs.

"You know, you should have just shot me," the cop said. "Because I'm going to eventually get free from here, and when I do."

"Who said I'm not going to shoot you?" I asked. "Or I could cut your throat, which would be quieter."

"Well, while you're thinking just how you're going to kill me, how about you pass me a butt."

His cigarettes were on the table. I tossed them over to him with some matches and he lit one and sat staring at us.

Ramona took my plate and went to the kitchen to wash up. I followed her.

"I found what they were hiding," I told her.

"What?"

"I found what you and Elmer made me follow them for."

"It was Elmer, not me. I didn't like the idea. I like you."
Her voice was like melted butter. "From when you first
walked in the door I liked you."

I told her that that is how I felt also, and then told her
that I had found it, what they had been looking for.

"I dug it up. It's in the car. We can leave here, together,"
I said. "We can go to Elephantine together."

"Elephantine?"

"Sure. We could be there in three or four days. Unless
something is keeping you here."

She looked down at the dirty plate and frying pan. "No,
nothing is keeping me here."

"Do you trust me?"

"Yes."

I told her I was tired and she said to lie down. She'd
finish washing up and keep an eye on the cop. I went into
her room. I'd seen it through the open door but hadn't
been in there before. The only furniture was a bed and a
dresser. There was a mirror on the dresser and a hair brush.
I lay down on the bed and closed my eyes. It felt good to
lie down. I fell asleep and woke up and fell asleep again. At
one point I thought I felt someone touching my face and
then opened my eyes and no one was there. A while later I
was just staring at the window.

Then things started to fade to white.

Brunilda Griego

Traditions virtues of anger just sat there and smelled the years go by a little girl pinching beetles old woman pinching beetles what is it they want of me three strong men no one looked at me when I was young but her they did yes not them but him I sat for three hours drinking coffee black as a crow without attachment of the heart she was making tortillas again a few of us all that was left no daughters to teach if we could teach theirs if I had let her if grandfather had not drifted away then three or four of them to carry things blood shot from his wounds mother had looked at the cracks in the sky she showed us how to roll into light tuck in your chin angry light I pinched Candelaria until her skin was between my fingers when it got dark we use the dark we went by we I mean me and my sister she hated it but she was born to it would die to it let her make tortillas forever we're old women too late to turn back now yes I pinched her until she bled I can hear him as he enters angry wisdom when grandfather died I had to do it he would not go away would never go away he taught me the secret mysteries the years smell like old food and forget me up there stopped digging there a long time ago he must be putting the knife into her now pinching her with the knife we look through glass windows everyday look through glass windows the black coffee always there in the outhouse the routes of the stars and their rays some lamp the bottom points the planet how to travel on them I still think of things everything turned within and from within we saw without ever and went off out the window down past the old goat he still knew who we were could never forgive us for the blood that had come spilling out so long ago grandfather cutting her throat us eating her meat and now we went through the trees the moon was in the sky like her tortilla the wind weak as it was blowing us along she behind me always behind me they were behind dirty moustaches waiting for us with their muscles and knives and noses when we got there no crowns of thorns for their heads when they saw me in the daytime the kingdom tumult of the flesh I pushed down on the insects he must be done now and coming this way just lay still they would bow their heads and look away gold is round not even look at our house but they would still come had come to life covered with slime and blood so they were crying blood like a grey wolf they kissed at me one at a time they did they wouldn't rape me grain is round everything is round I would never drown drifting no songbirds of pain once it was I visited the world under the sand where was he was grandfather there still drifting around I heard and looked they brought him the one who was off sleeping with Ramona we could have showed her I put a moonbeam between my legs we tried to but she was not interested what do you want was asked him what language was that he spoke hit him so hard that he passed out the first thing is darkness I came out of that they wanted to pinch his throat but I said no nail him up the nails went easily right through his hands chile running over a tortilla my door is opening now did they think rodents could make the love to a lantern force a lantern maybe they could her corporeal body he is standing over me was still a virgin foolish wisdom as a round ball did he sharpen the knife with saliva well it's going into me now dripping black coffee I am dripping black coffee.

Rudy Trujillo

Never trust a woman.

She sat there and watched me all night while he snoozed on her bed. When I tried to talk to her, she didn't reply. Even when I told her I needed the toilet she just sat there holding the gun joylessly.

I felt like hell. My head felt like it was stuffed full of cotton. My neck hurt. My back hurt and I had a cramp in my arm which was hooked up to that damned stove.

In the morning he left to get a car and while he was gone she made coffee and put a few things in a bag.

"I think you're making a mistake," I told her.

She still didn't reply.

"Look," I said, "it's not like I was going to rape you. I just wanted to pump you for information. I'm a cop. It's my job."

She was silent. Didn't even look at me and then he pulled up.

"Leave the gun," he told her. "It's only trouble."

She set it on the table and they each swallowed down a few sips of coffee. I didn't even bother asking for a cup. She took her bag and they went out.

I heard them driving off—not toward town, but north. I struggled. There wasn't much chance of getting free that way. I thought of calling out, but the only ones who might hear me were the old women across the road. And if they found me like that, who knew what they would do with me. I had heard tales.

I supposed I could have worked the stove loose and dragged it away with me, but dragging two or three hundred pounds of cast iron around didn't seem like much of a solution.

I had one butt left and lit it and just as I was exhaling my first drag I heard another vehicle pull up in front of the house. A car door slammed and then a moment later Elmer came in. He was carrying a crowbar. The morning was sure off to a good start.

"Hello there," I said.

He didn't answer. I licked my lips and went on:

"Um, listen, your aunt sort of locked me up. She locked me up and drove off with that guy. Do you think you could unlock me? I would really appreciate it if you could."

"You hurt me, boss."

"I know I did, Elmer. But you have to realize that I was just doing my duty. It was nothing personal. You have to realize that. I like you, Elmer, I really do."

He didn't reply but his hands were still tight around the crowbar and I didn't think it would give my hair quite the right part.

"Now, I don't know what your plans are for that crowbar, but killing or maiming an officer of the law could get you in a heck of a lot of trouble. Your aunt and Cleopatra, or whatever his name is, are already in trouble. Big trouble. I guess that treasure you were talking about is real. They have it and they drove off with it. North. They just left. Not ten minutes ago. We might still be able to catch them."

"We?"

"Sure, you want your aunt back, don't you?"

"And the treasure."

"And about half the treasure. The State needs to meet its expenses too, you know."

A sad sort of smile tugged at the corners of his mouth. He came over, still gripping the crowbar tight. I figured he was going to crack open my skull but then he dropped the crowbar and kneeled down.

"I don't have a key," he said, looking at the handcuffs.

"I know you don't. They took it and drove off. But there's a spare set in the glove-box of my car. If you could go out and get it and unlock me, I think we could mutually benefit each other. I'm a hell of a driver, and we could catch up with them. You get half the treasure and you get your aunt. I can't do nothing with her."

He went out to the car and came back a minute later with the spare keys.

"Go ahead and hand them over."

He did and I unlocked myself and got to my feet.

I stretched out my arms and cracked my back and pulled my freight up off the floor. My left wrist was sore and I rubbed it. His bottle of Frost 8/80 was on the table, almost full, so I took it and poured myself a long one. I put my gun in its holster. I popped two black beauties in my mouth and washed them down with a short one.

"What's that?" Elmer asked.

"Aspirin."

"I've never seen that color aspirin before, boss."

"They're extra strength."

I handed him the whisky bottle and he took a gulp.

It was light outside. I took a leak against the side of the house and then we climbed into the car and started off. I had heard them go north, so that's the direction we went. Some characters were there in the road jumping around and waving their arms so I swerved around them.

Cleopatra and Ramona had had about thirty minutes head start, but on that road there was nothing for about sixty miles and it was hard to go over twenty-five mph unless you were a maniac. I gunned it up to sixty in about a minute flat.

We flew out of the village and into a pine forest. The road was hell, but I'd go through hell to catch those two.

"Hey, slow down, boss," Elmer said. His hands were gripping at the dashboard.

"Relax, this is what I do for a living."

I twirled the steering wheel this way and that as we went around the bends. It was like I was Mario Andretti. A tornado of dust spilled off the back of the car. We whumped over a rise and then caught a little air as we came up over a hill. It must have been a nightmare on the shocks, but one thing about being an employee of the State is that they have to pick up the tab when I do my, um, duty.

I looked over at Elmer. He had some liquid cement in his hand and was putting it on a rag and sniffing it. I informed him of the illegality of his actions, but he just gazed at me blankly so I took a couple of pills and washed them down with Frost 8/80 Dry White Whisky and let

Elmer take a short pull.

Coming over a ridge, I saw some dust up ahead.

"That'll be them."

I eased up on the gas and floated along enough so I could see their heads. Some kid was staring out the rear window.

"Who's that?" I asked.

"Looks like the Montoya boy."

"I guess they swiped him. That's a first degree felony."

They drove, and I followed, on them like white on rice. They went faster and so did I, letting her out a little at a time, just to keep up. Because I wanted to get them, yes, but there would be time for that.

The pines were tall around there and that road, I knew, was seldom travelled.

I thought about taking a few pot shots at them as we drove, but shooting out of a car window while driving is a lot more difficult than one might think and those bullets cost money, taxpayer money, so I shouldn't waste them.

I looked over at Elmer next to me. He was high as a kite. Once I got the treasure, I'd waste him too and throw him off into the sagebrush. No use jailing a son of a bitch like that. Would just be one more expense the State didn't need.

"So what kind of treasure is it?" I asked him.

"Gold." He didn't sound too certain. "I think it's gold."

"Well, I guess it's got to be something."

I took a couple more beauties and another slug of Frost 8/80, which wasn't quite as smooth as Schenley, but still managed to quench my thirst. I let Elmer have another drop and then relieved him of the bottle and took another pull. I was starting to feel good. Really good.

I hadn't eaten since the hamburger the day before, but I wasn't hungry. Still, I'd have to eat. Man cannot live on pills alone. Once I got this business over with I would go home and shower and shave and go out and get some food. A big breakfast and coffee. After, maybe I would go over and see Gilbert and tell him I couldn't find his boyfriend. I'd stay on the job for a couple months just taking it easy. Then quit. Say I found God. Go down to Mazatlan and feed on beer and hookers for a couple of years.

Sun Hair

Who took off my arm pulling my leg are you ouch pulling it right off ouch ouch I was blue they were pulling ha ha them off ouch ouch he came in and thick wet threw it on me I started snacking retreat licked some off my lips what a taste wow I was laughing and a long time ago when I used to be in a garden drinking water a humming bird.

They were laughing while they did it stirred up the spirit on the look I'm a rabbit watch how I hop am a dog listen to me growl.

Table I flew into her and came out looking like this nothing like the taste of old wood she was crying and asked us to stop it just to back together tried to put it but it would not ha ha stay another he came in with a bucket of it and my eyes opened eating the holy thing opened.

Not too many feathers wide merry puzzle I could only ha ha laugh jumped over the chair and rug the under crawled she was crying so I went a whoring so I smile so I am a dog and move my arms very fast.

Wanted to lick her tears he was yelling the father was barking out funny sounds if I.

Slapped him on the back he would be a pam pam poom drum the others said they wanted to see the boy we wouldn't eat him just tear him to even smaller and I said the same we told him he had asked us what we wanted to the house I behold me smoking my pipe.

Rode my brother he was a horse slap him I be holding his hair I mean ha ha mule and I was a rider I mean rider kept when you say retreat we charge kept pushing down on the eggs with my feet but they just keep going faster remember when I went underground and pollinated the women down there.

I was so small they laughed at me got wet wonder if they make them with holes in the middle ha ha ha.

Or square so they can be stacked up like little bricks could build a house of eggs of castle I climbed down from the sky or should I say we did all for all landing on my hands and tumbling onto my feet then flowers came up from the earth they were jokes.

Cleopatra

The sky was turning that turquoise over the rim like something you could swim in. My head hurt, my hands hurt. I could feel a tooth loose in my mouth but then looked next to me and she was there. Well, she wasn't cheap, they could follow me all the way from Alexandria but they wouldn't find me, wouldn't find us and the sounds would disappear, the explosions, the turmoil. It was bad to treat a kid that way so I'd treat this one better finally some family maybe not perfect but I wouldn't care wouldn't walk up and down the street at night. Maybe I could forget, but something was still bothering me. I could look at it all I wanted to but it always stayed the same.

"What's the matter?" she asked.

"The gas gauge."

"It looks like we have plenty."

"It looks that way, but it hasn't moved since I nabbed this car yesterday. I've heard of cars with good gas mileage, but this takes the cake."

"So?"

"The car's new enough, but that gauge is broken."

"So we could run out?"

"At any time."

But I had only put about thirty or thirty-five miles on

it since the day before. And maybe the tank had started off full or pretty near full thinking of some camel its hump running out of water. How many miles would we have to get and could we get across the desert, make it to the temple?

"How far is it to Aswan?" I asked.

"To where?"

"Never mind."

Why make her worry. We were together and moving so there was nothing to worry about. A person can only control so much. Or maybe they can't control anything at all and maybe it's Amun-Ra who does it, makes all the decisions like playing with dolls. I opened the last bottle of terps and finished it in three long swallows.

"Who are you running from?" the kid said from the backseat.

"What makes you think we're running from someone?"

"Is it the Galaxy Club?"

I just shook my head could see him peering at me from back there just like he was a hallucination. He had a scrape on his forehead and maybe that had something to do with it. I still owed him five bucks. No matter how far you ran you were always in the same place, maybe the scenery is just changed and I was still the same kid looking out the window seeing him stalk by I could imagine being shut out from my own life my own child walking into villages and just shooting people it was fear that made us do that. Something that couldn't be forgotten because I had seen the looks on their faces their eyes when we did it just like the look of his face when he came to the door. It's easy to hurt people and maybe that's what being a hero is, seeing how many people you can hurt, how badly you can hurt them. He had told him to get out of there and I went back a long time later and she wasn't around just him 90-proof up to his eyeballs. He invited me in and served me a drink and we talked for an hour and I left and that was it, he said they had probably locked him up.

She asked me if I was alright.

"Sure." I grinned and she gave something like a smile in return.

I looked over my shoulder. He had fallen asleep, was probably exhausted.

"Are you sure we should take him with us?" she asked.

"Why not?"

"Kidnapping."

"He was wandering along the road. We're not holding him for ransom. He showed me where to dig it up."

"Is there a lot?"

"A big jar full. I owe him something."

"You're in charge."

"He's there, isn't he?"

"Of course he is."

Yes, the whole world was there and Ra could look down on it and the rain would come and that's how people were fed. I'd feed them us stalking through the rice paddies and then opening up and I'd grow fields of it and feed them making them grow hungry down there. Yes, I couldn't forget. And I had wounded people too and probably would never be forgiven. And I don't know what I thought I'd find. Trying to keep them from crossing the Nile and then

I opened my eyes and everything was shaking. The ceiling was shaking the bed was shaking and then I realized it was me and they were trying to hold me still.

Yes, he came to the door. Scotty wouldn't let him see me and Scotty told me what my name was. I said no but they changed it all the same that I couldn't carry the name of a lunatic like him so fine but I really am the Queen of the Nile someone laughed about that once and they still can't walk maybe never will again. Imagine being abandoned by your father but he hadn't otherwise he wouldn't have been walking out there with his gun. So the kid could help me. He was stretching himself back there now. He could hoe the ground.

"Are you scared?" she asked.

"No."

"I am."

Okay, so be scared. Then I looked in the rear view mirror and saw it.

Alfonso Torcuato Southerland-Hevia y Miranda

I am six foot six, well-built and good looking. It is not that I wish to brag, so much as to give an honest view of myself. Women often comment on the beauty of my eyes, which are the color of turquoise.

My life was never an easy one, but I have always done my best, and never complained about the hardships I have been beset with. My mother abandoned me at a young age, believing, in her madness, another to be her son. Even when he inherited all her goods and chattels, I accepted it without a murmur, clinging fast to the love in my heart and setting off on the adventure of life with nothing but the shirt on my back and, um, a single thin dime in my pocket.

I worked at a gum factory during the day and then at night took classes at the National Training Center for Lie Detection, afraid of nothing, least of all work. One evening when the wind was blowing in from the rocking sea, I was recruited by the Special Assessment Unit. I accepted the responsibility and scrambled around to complete my tasks.

I was taught how to use a pistol, and found that I was an excellent shot. Some people are naturally good at everything they do. I was one of them.

That I had made a success of my life was due to my

power of will, and my bloodline, as no one gave me a helping hand or even a friendly smile. Indeed, I had to work twice as hard as the rest, scooting as well as I could beneath the radar of their envy.

But, by nature, I do not grumble, so let us move on.

Just doing a service to this same man who had usurped my rightful place at the family table, I had driven up into the hills in order to have a discussion with a certain *Cleopatra* about some items he had extracted from my *brother's* possession.

Driving out, I had a few soft drinks which woke me up and put me in the right frame of mind to deal with the matter at hand.

I parked my Cadillac at the base of a gated driveway and got out. I walked down a long path which was flanked with statues of naked women, done in marble I believe, and lemon trees in large clay pots. I knocked at the door and about half a second later a Chavacano manservant answered. His lips were shiny and so red they looked like they had been painted. His eyes were strangely belligerent. Glancing down, I noticed that his shoes, though well-shined, were far from new. I explained that I was there to see the lady of the house, the Countess.

"She's not accepting visits," he replied in a thick foreign accent.

"I think she'd appreciate it if you told her I was here."

He grinned and shook his head and told me no.

I then hit——I mean firmly took him by the hand and gently explained why I found his behavior to be in need of rectifying. We talked about anger and how it was a natural emotion, but that he shouldn't let it get the better of him.

"I'm here for an important reason," I told him. "You're a good looking young man. There's no reason why you can't be nice to me and do your employer a favor at the same time. We might all become friends. You could always depend on me."

He seemed persuaded. He hugged me tightly and, while crying on my shoulder, admitted that he had been in the wrong. He said that he would fall in love with me if he were a woman and suggested that if I ever wished to sleep with his sister, he would arrange it. Slipping him a five and a few cigarettes, I suggested he withdraw. He then climbed into an old but well-maintained Chevy which was parked in the driveway and, waving his hand in gratitude, drove away.

I entered. The place was decorated in too effusive a manner for my taste. The windows were shielded by primrose macramé curtains. Some brightly-colored French paintings hung from the walls. The Countess was standing at the base of the stairway, the curves of her body inviting me forward.

She was wearing a yellow dress of some kind of soft material. It was low cut, but not too low cut. As soon as we were inside, she started peeling it off, but I asked her to wait. Her eagerness embarrassed me.

"Kiss me," she said. "Please kiss me."

I chucked her gently under the chin. Poor child. I could give her happiness that night, but the next morning she would be more miserable than ever. I had a life to lead and could only lead it in my own way, unencumbered by emotional, er, baggage.

"Fix me a drink," I said.

"And then later we can make love?"

"If you're good I might."

She gently squeezed some lemon in a glass, added some vermouth and a few frigid cubes of ice, and stirred it with her pinky. She poured herself a stiff one of straight bourbon but it was gone before she got to me.

I sat down on the edge of a chair and sipped my drink with caution. I was afraid I was giving her the wrong idea. I often seem to do that—give women the wrong idea. I have always been a little too friendly. That is one of my personality flaws. She nestled up to me, pushed herself onto my lap. If she had been carrying a suitcase full of bricks, she still wouldn't have weighed more than a little girl. I smiled sadly and kissed her on the forehead.

"What would make you happy?" I asked. The least I could do was seem to care.

"Having a big strong man like you to look after me. I'd do anything you wanted."

I believed her.

I smoothly lifted her off my lap and set her down on the divan. I didn't know whether I should give her a few hours of splendid joy, or not. In the end, I decided to be generous. After all, I regularly made donations to about fifteen charitable organizations, why not to her as well? Even wealthy nymphomaniacs deserve a certain amount of pity.

When I kissed her, she writhed like a snake split in half with a sword. Her teeth chattered under my touch. I tried to calm her and informed her that I was, after all, a man and not a machine, but she was too fresh to understand what I was saying.

Finally, after a prolonged length of time, I was able to unlatch her from me. I removed myself to a chair and began lacing my shoes. She was giving me a pleading look that I pretended not to notice.

It was then that he walked in and I rose to greet him. I stuck out my hand to shake his, but slipped and fell and ended up knocking the poor man over. I tried to help him up, but he kept knocking his face against my, um . . .

Er.

Yes, for some reason he wouldn't shake my hand or look me in the eyes. He felt ashamed. I could tell that much. I told the Countess to get us some glasses of lemonade, and he nodded his head. His lips were trembling. He felt that nervous.

I tried to talk to him, but it was difficult.

The glasses of lemonade arrived. He set his on a table. I put mine to my lips and drank half of it at a swallow. It tasted rather bitter. A few moments later, everything started to get blurry. I rubbed my eyes. Was it because I couldn't love her? That was the only reason I could think of as I slid onto the floor.

How long was I out for? I couldn't say. When I came to, Elmer, the Chavacano manservant, was kneeling next to me wetting my lips with brandy. My head felt like an echoing corridor.

"A cigarette," I murmured.

He lit a Newport and put it in my mouth. I took a few

puffs and remembered.

"We have to get them," I said.

Two minutes later we were in my Cadillac Coupe de Ville.

My foot eased down on the pedal and we began to pick up speed, going up to around ninety mph, which was rather fast for that road. But they hadn't seemed to want to wait for me, so I was forced to throw caution to the wind. We snaked rapidly through the hills, my hands turning the wheel as if I had been dancing the cha-cha-cha with Carmen Miranda.

Elmer, the Chavacano manservant, was agitated. It was clear that he had no rhythm. I could see large pearls of sweat standing out on his face. He looked like the Sulu Archipelago. I felt like patting him on the shoulder and telling him not to worry, but I didn't.

"The money is mine," he told me. He grinned, but he was anything but happy. "I've been working for her for almost ten years. She's only been giving me twenty-five cents a day. Then I discovered the treasure while weeding the flower bed. No one would have known about it if it hadn't been for me. It's mine."

I shook my head.

"No," I said. "It isn't yours. You can have part of it, but the whole thing would do you more harm than good. You need a new pair of shoes. You need nourishment. You need to send your sister to typing school. But having too much would do you more harm than good."

He laughed uneasily. "And you?"

"I'm not doing this for the money."

His eyebrows went up as if he were asking me what I was doing it for.

Poor fellow. It was no fault of his that he was ignorant and could never understand a generous heart like mine. Growing up I had had even less opportunity than him, but I couldn't expect the whole world to be like me, to rise above their situation and surroundings. Most people were weak. They needed my compassion. I had to keep my mouth shut. I would give him his share of the money. And the rest I would donate to the Oceanside Christian Children's Foundation. I would put it in an envelope and slip it under their door early in the morning, before anyone was awake. They would wonder who put it there, but they would be grateful. Every now and again I would drive by and watch the children playing happily in the playground, swirling through the air on their swings, but I would do it without ostentation.

Thinking of it made me smile.

Up ahead I could see the other car. He was driving dangerously fast and I feared his skills were not as great as mine. I felt like calling out and telling him that there was no need for him to take such risks. He was his own worst enemy, not I.

When I caught up with him, and I would catch up with him, I would explain. I only hoped he would listen. I bore him no grudge and was willing to forgive. I only hoped he was willing to be forgiven.

Yes, he had been unkind to my *brother*, and even more unkind to me. He had something that did not belong to him. It belonged to the children. Surely he would understand that the children needed it more than he did, but I also realized that in this world selfishness is king. I had been chained up by naked women in their cellars and arm wrestled at gun point for my life.

Working for the Special Assessment Unit, nothing was new to me.

I suppose he thought that by kidnapping the Countess, he could use her as a hostage. And possibly use her in other ways too. It is for this reason that I had insisted on remaining emotionally unentangled. The time I had found myself in bed with the Pan-Am stewardess in a Hilton Hotel in Tanzania had taught me that much.

Elmer, the Chavacano manservant, took a bottle from his pocket and then took a drink. A long one. I shuddered. Was he an alcoholic?

The Galaxy Club

There are five of us all fun some cretins maybe but better laugh tears flying from your eyes you'll laugh don't ask where we come from because we've even forgotten just look at our grins and hope we don't bite you we mean kiss you hey ho. Laying about with our legs in the air trying to annoy sitting on each other smothering one another sneaking over to L 5 Flower and seeing him sleep what a benevolent big fellow a shame his thoughts are so unrestricted while ours are twisted to good humor watch us flip stuff a cloud in your ear ouch allow us to bite off your quit sucking on our hair from one to the next a big circle.

Wrapping rainbows around our heads knee up to chin hop on one leg better than that one who's always got his tongue hanging out it's long enough to fall to the ground what's that a mile.

We're heads dogs legs dogs did you ever hear the one about the rabbit with a wistful voice.

We're dogs but never trust the Coyote did we say never trust the Coyote Ferox and we never did trust him hard to trust a fellow who copulates with trees oh wait we do that too ha ah ha it was his idea to give Blue Boy life in the first place it was a bad joke and we let them have their way knowing it would be more fun later when we could take him back when we spit from the sky do you look up. What was that oh when Our Little Lady of the Trunk complained with her grievous groan when the Virgin complained with her groan her panting breast one of us behind and she screamed and cried out and slapped us away as if taken her maidenhood we may so the wind didn't blow that day even a few drops of rain we mean spit.

And this was after the fish we mean dragons had come forgetting themes of love you might say demanding Blue Boy's execution head roll hup! kick it over the moon kick it away from his little body as fast as you can.

"Better let us take him by the arms. And feet. And hair. And rip him," we said and nobody laughed but we for it would be such a funny joke to set his crying mother free and we whistled.

"Well, he took my arm and look at my head," the Virgin complained and Coyote said to wait wait he'd spring some blood from the cradle but never trust the Coyote right so down he went so it was play and peace for a little while plucking at mist rolling over each other did you ever hear the one about the girl who stood under the rain and got the men beastly drunk through the forests we can ride over the clouds we can fly and things went like this until later Coyote came back holding a neat little piece of lavender scalp saying he had eaten him.

"Doubtful!" we all shouted, none of us believed him since liar detects liar and we decided to give him our strongest star tequila like we were the girl in the rain our eyebrows flying in every direction as we offered it and he drank and we played and toyed with each other's noses and served him more now his mouth going both east and west have you ever seen the Coyote smile juice seventy trillion tons of stars and allow them to ferment for about a thousand years.

It was good. We asked if he wanted more. Yes, he did licking his lips baring his teeth toddling around on two legs and falling to four another taste yes another puke up now no not yet well take another swallow.

"So you ate the Blue Boy?"

"Was he good?"

"Delicious."

"Another drink?"

"Yes."

There is grief in the ha but mirth in the killing ha ah ha so down his throat we poured it did you ever hear the one about the man who shod his horse the wrong way well what goes down had to come up and he threw up the goat and so we knew he hadn't eaten the Blue Boy and we kicked Coyote in his side and threw him about and then like water poured from a jug went down each one jumping when our feet hit the earth and everything was twinkling with morning.

We went through the town snatching up bits of dog excrement and eating them playing leap frog peeing in the street. When we found the little fellow we would tear him limb from limb. Doing somersaults humping the ground. Some of us walk backward some of us chop at fruit trees chairs anything with our hands and our heads. Getting the chickens and flattening out their eggs with our feet and then to the other side oopla through the window another crashing backward through the door.

"He in there?"

"No. Just a dead woman."

"Same here my honey and my sweet!"

"So."

"Where is he?"

"He isn't here."

"Where?"

"There"

"Near?"

Two of us jumped on the backs of two and one led the procession and we galloped up the road. Some vegetable garden and we ran through tearing up the vegetables and throwing them at each other pulling up some bean plants. Now walking on hands now wriggling along like a worm along the daisied ground the sun was leaking on us would wipe it up but we only had rags.

Then we got to the old man's house and his wife came out to sport and play one of us wrapped himself around her leg she cried out how disgusting how disgusting us screaming about love's courtship fresh cheese and cream falsely weeping lips twisted hands clasped like beggars' bow wow dog-like bark, "O cow o cow where is the rich farmer's son?"

And then the man came along. He came forward, we went backward, puffing out our cheeks.

"What do you want?" he demanded.

His eyes were charming!

"Where is the boy where is the boy give him to us!"

He yelled at us and told us to get out of there and

our teeth started chattering which he liked and each of us laughed louder than the next throwing arms in the air rubbing bellies opening mouths wide twang twang.

"He's been a bad boy we need to take him from you eat him up so sorry."

"He isn't here. He's my son, but he isn't here."

She cried, "Make them go away!"

The dew was coming from her eyes now fast and we love the dew do you inspiration going from anus to anus and we decided together that even if he wasn't in the house we had better look though we hated to be thorough and through the house we stormed, upsetting tables, chairs, leaping up and down on the beds in the bedrooms, sticking head in cabinet, arms under rugs, groping around, in the kitchen eating and drinking everything spilling what we didn't eat or drink, twirling plates on our fingers, breaking glasses.

She was crying and asked us to stop it we asked her if her hills of snow she'd show so she ran needed more mischief, shake and wink.

We tried to put the broken dishes back together, but they would not stay, the pieces falling off as soon as they were on, now trying to fit the pieces in our eyes and ears but they wouldn't fit.

"Better eat it!"

One of us started eating a plate, another a broken glass, a third trying to chew on the table. That way and this. One of us curtsied. We still can't remember when we were born. Our mother she didn't talk did you ever hear the one about the dog who had rabies and was killed with a scythe one in one room another in a chamber the poor old couple would lose their ha ha ha.

The house we went through carrying kettles and pans one throwing apples targets sounding, laughing, licking the walls.

Here how where?

Wait there he we is blue kill blue there he there he ouch ouch ouch a screech loss of blood we must hop and leap did you ever I have an arm I have a leg but it won't stick back on.

Ramona Roybal

Maybe I was making a mistake but I didn't care. To stay would have been a mistake too. Sometimes everything is a mistake and you just hope you're making the right one.

"We have enough gas to go a couple of hundred miles," he said looking at the gauge. "It gets good mileage."

A couple of hundred miles. Away from my house me just leaving it with the policeman in there handcuffed to the stove. But how much longer could I have lasted anyhow? Soon there wouldn't be anything left. I hadn't been pretty for a few years. Maybe even longer. Maybe since I was a child. At least I had been a pretty child.

But then a woman. It's never easy to be alone. I looked out and saw the trees moving past us and imagined us going on like that forever.

Then he started saying something. He was worried. Maybe there wouldn't be a couple of hundred miles because the gas gauge was broken and we talked a little and Blue Boy piped in from the back seat. Were we running? It seemed like Cleopatra smiled so everything would be alright.

It had to be. I couldn't stand to have another man shot or sitting listening to the wind. Just watching the lights parade past. And it seemed like my whole life had already been but also never really happened the trees moving by us me thinking that wherever he got the car we'd have to leave it somewhere sometime.

I looked at Blue Boy in the back seat. He was asleep now holding his stick like it was a doll. Why were we taking him? Yes, that was a mistake too. I guess Cleopatra had love in his heart and he was trying to give it to everybody.

I didn't have it for everybody.

And I didn't have it for Elmer and never would. Feeling sorry, maybe even liking, but not really liking very much, isn't love and maybe this was my last chance at it, at something that might, just might, be happiness.

He had been sleeping and I bent over. His face felt rough. At least he respected me. Only I hoped he wouldn't respect me too much then I looked in my side mirror and saw it and asked him if he was scared and he said no.

"He's behind us."

"Yes."

I looked over my shoulder.

"How did he get loose?"

"I don't know, but he's after us."

There was someone else in the car with him. I looked hard for a minute, light glaring off the window but then I could see. By the outline it looked like Elmer.

"Elmer's with him," I said.

"Well, that explains how he got loose."

I felt like crying but I didn't. I looked at Cleopatra. His face was the same, but I knew he was worried. I reached out and touched his hand and he squeezed mine and then let go and put it back on the steering wheel. He was concentrating on the driving and I felt that maybe, just maybe, he could do it.

He pressed down on the gas pedal and we started going faster. The dust was boiling behind us so I couldn't really see the police cruiser any more but felt like something was trying to grab me from behind.

Theodore Montoya

A long time ago my father would tell me about all sorts of things. About men coming down from the sky and causing wars. About sheep who could gamble and rabbits that ate children. I would sit and listen but never felt afraid. The neighbors used to speak of the Devil. He lived in a place near Candelaria's. His place was the smallest around. So many of them went to him. But in this life I've spent more time with my cows than with men.

Yes, my father told me about many things.

Perhaps that is why I was never too surprised.

That morning Blue Boy hadn't come out to breakfast. Ibbie checked his bed. It had been slept in, but he was nowhere in sight. She was worried.

"He's probably playing down by the creek," I said.

I went to look after the cows. I passed by the creek but didn't see Blue Boy. He was getting into trouble somewhere probably. Catching more fish that were not too good to eat. I smiled when I thought of the one we had had for dinner a couple of nights before. A real dinner of bones.

The cows acted strange that morning and were all pressed against the northern side of the pasture. I guess they sensed something but I don't know what. I heard a vehicle move up the road. Hardly anyone went that way, that early.

On my way back I detoured to the Griegos' goat pen. He sometimes liked to feed the old goat. He wasn't there and neither was the goat. There was just a big hole and my shovel laying next to it. Then I knew something was up. That goat had been there for longer than any goat should, and it was gone.

I picked up the shovel and headed back home and there they were, bothering Ibbie.

They were ugly and foolish-looking, with white heads and big black eyes. Lips just forming a round outlet, but a couple had sharp teeth. One had a long nose. Ibbie was naturally frightened. Perhaps I should have been too, but I was too old to be frightened of such things. A long time ago other men had come to my door. It was during summer also. They had said I should go with them to the morada. That I should bring with me money and candles. I hadn't gone. For two weeks they had come walking around the house late at night. Then one came to my door. It was Ezequiel Baca. He was old and shrewd-looking. We talked for a while, about the heat and about a cow I had slaughtered. He told me I should go with him, but I just shook my head. He went away and then they stopped coming around.

I understood Blue Boy liked to cause trouble. But I also understood that he was my son. Just thinking that was strange, because in a way I had always felt that he was not part of me. Not that I knew what was a part of me. Just my memories. And I had had a lot of those before he was even born.

We were probably too old for him, but I wouldn't let them hurt him. Perhaps I shouldn't have set out the liquor on the stone. Perhaps I should have just accepted things since I had already accepted so much. But when you do something you have to take responsibility.

They were tearing up the house. Ibbie was crying.

I had a rifle and could have shot them, but somehow I imagined that wouldn't help much. Bullets are for men and sometimes animals, but they didn't seem to be either.

They were walking backwards. One was chewing on the edge of the table, another smashing crockery against himself. Yes, better leave the gun alone. They would just laugh probably. They were too crazy to be hurt like that.

I had to figure out another way.

A long time ago, when I was a boy, my father had told me, "If someone is stronger than you, be more clever than them."

They were looking for my son and if they found him they would hurt him. That much was clear.

I scratched my head and had an idea.

So I went out to the shed. The paint was still there. I had been planning on starting that day. I took a screwdriver and pried off the top of a can, stirred it up with a stick and then carried it toward the house. I told Ibbie to go away, to stay in the garden.

They were running around creating all sorts of noise. Always laughing but there was nothing really funny. They had already broken the place up pretty well. One was eating the rug in the living room now. Causing a lot of damage. It was the one with the long nose. I was starting to feel pretty angry.

"Look at this," I said and when he looked up with big blank eyes I took the bucket of paint and splashed some over him. It went on his face and nose and ran down his chest. He stood still in surprise. I lifted up the bucket and poured the rest over his head.

I don't think he knew what it was, what I was doing, but then he started gurgling laughter. I dropped the can and stepped back.

"He's here," I called out. "He's here!"

The other four came in.

"Do you want Blue Boy?" I said. "He's right there." And I pointed.

Spittle was dripping out of their round mouths as two grabbed him by the arms and two of them by the legs and they started pulling. He was laughing while they pulled him apart. I could hear his bones crack but he kept laughing. There were feathers in the air. It was an ugly sight and I turned away. Turned and walked out of the house.

Ibbie was in the garden, wiping her eyes.

She asked me about Blue Boy. She asked me if they would take him away.

"Well, they won't take him away," I said. "But I don't know where he is."

She told me to find him.

Elmer Roybal

Out of one eye.

Is she with him he said she was with him if he took her took it and her I have to get them back I can hear something in my ears telling me that but he is sitting next to me driving but his lips aren't moving some glue burning burning hot. The pines are running by but let them run as fast as they want to I can win this I can win it is she with him.

"Is she with him?"

"I told you she was. They're in love. I don't know what they see in him, but they see something. But when I catch him . . ."

"They?"

"Don't ask."

"We split the money."

"Sure. One for you, two for me."

My head is like a paper bag after I'll hit him when he isn't looking we take it and go to the ocean I'll hit them both. I'm not looking at him now but ahead at the dust of the other car I'll explain to her how it has to be us walking in the sand by the ocean. The ocean. I once heard it in a shell I take out the cement. Just take a puff.

"What the hell," he says as I'm smelling.

"It's legal."

"Don't tell me about the law. There's nothing legal about it. Article 39. No person shall intentionally smell, sniff or inhale fumes or vapors."

Then he's putting another couple of those black aspirin extra strength in his mouth and tipping back another drink. Frost 8/80 Dry White Whisky. I could try to get his gun, but won't yet he's offering me the bottle but before I can hardly take a sip he's yanking it back rear tires sliding as he turns I've got the mineral deficiency I found it knew it was there didn't find it but knew it was there all for me nothing for you sometime I'll reach for it take one chance one chance I have to just take that one chance been too cautious always you slept on the floor by her bed it wasn't sleeping just staring at her in the dark she was scratching her arm and you were staring at her I am not your friend finally I'm up and then he gets her I brought him and he gets her. Now we're out of the forest, out of the hills. Flat see the plateau of sagebrush out of one eye. It's still early. The road stretches out no one's on it just them and us. I ask him why he doesn't pull them over.

"Just take it easy. Everything is going to happen in due course."

They're flying. We're flying shrubs squatting forever and above a giant sheet of blue daylight. Now my eye sees the chasm like the earth is cracked in two. Let's fly over it.

They're stopped why are they stopped. They're stopped she's going to see me coming up in this car feel like ducking I'll crawl under the bed so when she comes in.

Kill him.

I don't even know who. Eat this cement first to steady the nerves. He's doing his thing we're sitting just sitting on the top of nothing.

The Blue Boy is with them. Montoya's kid. I remember what she told me, what the Virgin told me so just get out and follow him take a chance my hand feels like a wing.

It is a big jar and I look inside gold gold what was it go——

"Jesus," the cop says.

"It's."

"I see what it is."

"That boy, he broke up the Virgin?"

"I really do hate hurting people, Elmer."

"He broke her up, he has to be stopped. The pistol."

"Are you as crazy as I am?"

"Let me see it, boss."

He's holding I'm pushing she's going away she was taller than me and I started to get taller and she got smaller it was hard to even talk when she was around then Serafin got shot or is that me and she was alone in the house I drank coffee and she was looking at me if I could only explain she had a job in town to come one night and I did and then they said never return because the funds were missing I say I didn't take them boss but I did and after I was outside on the sky the ground and they were kicking me but I couldn't feel I'm looking up at the sky for a while and then her car broke I drove her a few times and then she stopped going just the food stamps if we only had money but I knew I'm looking down into the ocean I can hear it there was it lots of it thought there was would work it out it's too late now though understand don't understand why did you do that to me a big spear is coming from the sky and I'm grabbing on to it is that you Serafin I can see through my other eye again.

Blue Boy Montoya

They say I cause trouble.

I wasn't scared of what the Coyote had told me, but I didn't want to cause problems for Mom and Dad. I'd go away for a while and come back. My stick could have smashed up the Galaxy Clowns, but they were already upset with me for beating up those fish. I had killed four of them, but Dad had said they were inedible and threw them on the compost.

I got up before Dad and got dressed. Mom was still asleep, so I poured myself a glass of milk and drank it. Then I took my Demon Taming Stick and went outside. It was still dark with a little glow coming over the mesa. The stars laughed at me but I didn't laugh back. They would be gone soon. So I started walking. First across the meadow, then along the creek, and it laughed at me and I stuck my tongue at it. Then it was light and I walked through it and over and up to the road. I had gone down it a few times with Dad but never remembered going up it where the trees were bigger. I went up the hill wishing I could hit something with my stick and walked and walked singing and poking the ground with my stick. I walked and walked and it seemed like the road went on forever. Then a car came along.

"Where are you going?"

I told him I was going away. He still owed me five dollars, but I didn't care so I didn't say anything.

He said I could get in and I did. Ramona didn't seem to like that, but she was still nice and we were going. I wondered if we were running from the Galaxy Club and asked them, and there were the little things on the back seat and a paper bag and I was collecting them and putting them in the bag, shave a pig, gathering hairs to make a wig.

The car moved and as it moved I closed my eyes. Maybe it was a long time ago, but I was very high up and could curl up under the sun and stay warm. I already missed the creek. Missed the mud and missed working with the mud and digging holes. Just collecting the kernels. My eyes opened and I stood up to look out back at the house but just saw an ugly car and so lay back down. The pig flew up in the air and the mouse married a bumblebee. I was jumping along with the flowers hitting them with my Demon Taming Stick. Hitting a big tree with my Demon Taming Stick and it was running away.

Then I opened my eyes. We were stopped.

"I want to go back home," I said.

"We can't do that now. We're out of gas."

Maize

They buried you here a long time ago. They were living up in the canyon and buried you thinking they would come back later when the land was open again. But the land never became open again and you stayed there in the cool earth.

Time.

You were sleeping. Dreaming. Distant past. Your body was one then. But you spread your arms and told the woodpeckers what to do. So they pecked you into pieces and carried you here and there. The birds. The grasshoppers.

You fed the men. Every day you did. The torn up pieces of your legs. Eating your scabs but they didn't know it. Good for them. Let them grind up your scabs. Called nourishment. Don't tell them where you got it.

Everything is slow. Until it happens.

The sound is there. Above. Above. You coming? I'm here, waiting for you. Hurry. All the time is nothing.

Now stopping. Don't give up. Could be. No. Coming again. Can almost feel the air. Waited this long, can wait a little longer. Yes. You are too used to waiting.

His hands are on me. On this thing that surrounds me. Now. Air. It's wonderful. Around you thick and sweet. See the sun. Want to soak in it throw out your arms. You are smiling. No one can see, because you have no lips. But you are smiling. One thousand of them.

This is a waking dream.

She spilled you and you turned her into a dog. She ground you up and spilled you. Couldn't let that go. How did it feel to be a dog?

Now is all you need is a drink. A long drink to clear it all up.

Moving. Horse? No, times. Spring. Recoil. Give you water so your hair will grow. It will grow long and yellow. Yes, the sun will spill through your hair and you will vomit your teeth. Just respect that.

An open field. Wind blowing through you. The season. Long days just feeling it. You can see the fingertips of light. Kiss you. Wondering how much does a rainbow weigh. When it rains.

You can wait. Impatiently. A big sweep of wind some sound of anxiety. Your body will be covered in a green cape.

He is looking at you. He is touching you. His greedy hands are feeling your breasts. Can wait a hundred years, two hundred years, two thousand but people stay the same. Maybe even worse.

He is touching me with blood.

Put my heart in the earth and I will love you digging in at the hooves.

Rudy Torcuato Southerland-Hevia y Miranda y Trujillo

Their car sat parked in the middle of the lane on the bridge. That was a violation right there. I pulled up about twenty yards behind it and cut off the ignition no sirens lights nothing. I tried to remember what I had been hired to do and for a few seconds said nothing but then shook my head if the government had hired me to get them I'd better do it.

"Well, there they are."

"I can see," he replied curtly.

I smiled but without warmth.

They were getting out of the car leaving our proximity. Trying to defect. I put the bottle to my lips and took a short one and then, um, a long one, and then another, this time pretty short. I hadn't had a repast light or otherwise and it was bombs away. I was feeling pretty good and just needed to focus the thing out until the end.

It wasn't about him any more and not sure it ever had been.

A generous heart like mine. Growing up I had hurt him. It looked to me like I just couldn't expect the whole God-damned world children playing happily people always trying to find out what I do for a living only hoped he would listen. I bore him no that road, I knew, was seldom winding down to the seaside wouldn't even write him a ticket hoped he was willing to be forgiven at them as we, okay we were stopped now and I would get it and then kayoe this other bastard or else leave no witness but shooting out. There was a pause. I probably swallowed too many. I could see them walking. They were snuckered up with their love child in tow.

I had lean good looks.

He had been unkind than one might think and those bullets something that did not belong to him understand the children need it more high as a kite the blue ranges towering up in the distance. Menace scuttled up my spine.

I took a deep breath. I hadn't eaten anything since that measly hamburger, I mean fillet mignon, the day before and a handful of beauties no wonder I wasn't hungry. Then we got out and started walking toward it as they were walking away.

Down below the ocean roared. Waves splashed against the shore. A gentle breeze blew in and I could see the sails of the, um, fishermen out at sea.

"She's leaving," he said tensely.

"I already told you."

I couldn't blame her. For one thing I had been unkind—for her own sake of course. I took a stiff one, lifting the bottle lithely up to my mouth and realizing that, in the end, I was a practical man God the bottle smelled good.

They were receding as fast as we were coming but I could get them at any time. When I was eighteen I used to shoot the neighbors' cats with a rifle. Gilbert and tell him I couldn't find his what if you oh it no no oh yes you little so. Did I mention my love of duty? Well, it is not that I wish to brag, so much as to have to do my duty get real with people. Now part of that comment on the beauty of my eyes which beaten the heck out of Elmer. The good of the community. I have a stack of diplomas a foot high.

I sighed. I sweated.

It was a case of theft. And I have always done my best, and I hate hurting people. Even when he inherited all I felt it so I had no choice. They walked on, and I didn't follow or did I pick up speed, going up to her out a little at a time, just to keep up that road. But they didn't seem to want to wait like white on rice there would be a time for that time for everything just another smell of the bottle.

That's all they used to eat and now we've got dry white whisky. The desert of drinks. The Sahara of booze. I opened the front door of the car and popped the trunk and went around. Elmer was already looking and I peered down. There was a big jar and it was spilling out.

The clouds were tall around there and I felt like patting him on the shoulder and I thought of taking a few. It was a big vase, Cherokee I imagine though maybe Spanish, what the hell do I know.

His teeth began chattering as he looked down. I followed his gaze world selfishness is king off into the sagebrush. No use jailing a son of a took a bottle from his pocket expense the state didn't need. Was he a dipsomaniac? I asked him. The car sat parked in the middle. I had been hired for the mission. I braced myself. Down below the ocean roared this business over with I would go home and his teeth began chattering after maybe I would go over and see I reached into my pocket my hip mother always liked you better kill money I'd waste him too and throw bitch like that. Would just be one more and then took a drink. A long one. It slid down my throat. I shuddered. Hadn't had my repast I mean, um, breakfast. I got waves splashed against the shore. Shower and shave and go out and get down. I followed his gaze.

I felt it with my hand. The kernels ran out onto the road, the light catching them so they almost sparkled. Gold like hell. Okay so probably some old chief planted it there. Sure people made money off of it, lots of it. Pig feed. Tamales.

There was one long one left in the bottle and I drank it and then chucked the bottle into the abyss. Over the bridge into the, um, ocean.

My body was raining sweat. Now I hate hurting people. I really do. But that Elmer had made me do it, had left it so I had no choice. And now that I had hurt him, it looked to me that I would just as well finish the job.

I reached in my pocket my hip felt what if you oh it no no oh yes you little so she always liked you better.

"What are you doing, boss?"

I looked at him. They were walking away. At the end of the bridge. I could just. He was coming. I just.

Red Willow Gorge

The river rushes through my hands and wind blows through my eyes. In the distant past I turned around, fingers reaching north, toes extending south. I move slowly. Slowly opening up opening endlessly up speaking one constant song of time of erosion of smooth sadness. Look down, my big smile.

It isn't sleeping. But I don't feel awake. Some calm drunkenness or meditation electrifying bolt frozen, slowly dissolving or maybe some constant weeping my teardrop bounces forever my teardrop is not navigable, it you cannot ford. Leap over me, you can't, slide over me you bird with extended wings.

My walls are deep.

The wind sighs through me. To the ocean I go always marching but never feel. I am on public show but they never came never looked at me never talked to me I am here I see you the way of the watercourse.

There is a hair that goes across my head. People roll over it. Sometimes they stop, lean over and look at my beauty my beauty unbounded I am beaming can you feel my mouth. The sad ones sometimes throw themselves off. And the wind blows through my eyes yes they frown.

But even the happy ones usually seem sad. Their thin

laughter gets lost in my nose but I am so gentle. To cradle you in my teardrop I don't want. No I won't sneeze it would take a million years.

Once someone, a poacher, threw off the heads of deer, bobcats, cougars, and a bear. And they fell into my lap. Crying. And they sat rotting in my eye. The spirits danced a circle on the cloud. Loosened boulders fell.

The hunters came.

Nothing can ever fill me if you have so many soft feathers.

It stopped in the middle. There were three inside, so very small and I am so large but see with the long eye. The eager whisper of morning. They must be cautious. The wind sighs through me.

The other two came. Some carriage of metal. More hound it isn't a bear head they want to throw. The world is meeting here. From high up L 5 Flower is looking but half asleep drooping so far.

A sound resonates again and again my echo is so lonely. My echo. I see you the way of the watercourse. They call that desire. The wing is in the sky.

You sun you are the hole above me.

Ramona Roybal

I was sitting there looking out the window. It was afternoon. He wasn't back yet. I could see the corn. Bright green, reaching up toward the sky. Looking at it made me feel like covering my face, but I didn't.

When I'd heard the shots I thought I was going to die. But I wasn't and didn't want to look to see if he was there. But he was. I didn't want to look back. Then I heard the boy running up behind us. We kept walking.

Blue Boy had pulled him by the hand. Said he'd brought something and gave him the sack. Then the police car screamed by. He swerved a little and seemed like he tried to hit us, but he didn't. He was alone in it now and flew down the road until he was out of sight.

Cleopatra looked in the sack and at me and the boy. The sun was up now and our shadows stretched behind us.

Then in the distance we could see a vehicle. It was a pick-up truck. The boy said it was his father's and a couple of minutes later Theodore drove up, behind the boy. He didn't get out or cut off the ignition but just sat there letting it idle. I looked at him but didn't wave, wondering if he was angry, but not really caring. I shouldn't have to be lonely. Cleopatra gave Blue Boy five dollars, then the boy turned around and walked to the truck and got in.

We kept walking. He took my hand and held it tight.

I was looking out at the corn. Felt it kick. That made me feel like crying too. Happiness I suppose. Though I still don't even know if I was happy. Remembering the dream. Elmer. He was bloody and stuffed himself down my throat. Hard to be happy thinking about that.

No, I wasn't happy or sad. Just sitting there. But I did like looking at it, the corn, watching it as it grew and reached higher and higher toward the sky. Like some kind of poem.

I was beginning to feel hungry. I had had a cheese sandwich for lunch, but was already feeling hungry.

I'd get up. Pretty soon I'd get up.

It was green outside. That should have made me happy. But somehow. Living all your life in a certain environment. Lots of things were living. But the living weren't the only things that lived. It was kicking. Maybe it would want to go home. The places he talked about I'd never heard of. I just sat there and looked out the window until I heard him coming.

About the Author

Brendan Connell was born in Santa Fe, New Mexico, in 1970 and was raised in part in rural Northern New Mexico. He has had fiction published in numerous places, including *McSweeney's*, *Adbusters*, and the World Fantasy Award winning anthologies *Leviathan 3* (The Ministry of Whimsy 2002), and *Strange Tales* (Tartarus Press 2003). He has had a number of novels and short story collections published, which include *Metrophilias* (Better Non Sequitur, 2010), and *Lives of Notorious Cooks* (Chômu Press, 2012).

CPSIA information can be obtained at www.ICGtesting.com
Printed in the USA
LVOW06s1617030614

388433LV00004B/445/P

9 781907 681257